AND THEN YOU DIE

AND THEN YOU DIE

An Aurelio Zen Mystery

MICHAEL DIBDIN

Pantheon Books New York

ISBN 0-375-42188-2

www.pantheonbooks.com

Printed in the United States of America

First American Edition
2 4 6 8 9 7 5 3 1

TO LUCA MERLINI

CONTENTS

VERSILIA

Aurelio Zen was dead to the world. Under the next umbrella, a few desirable metres closer to the sea, Massimo Rutelli was just dead.

The two men were different in just about every other respect too. Zen was wearing a short-sleeved cotton shirt, lightweight wool trousers and leather sandals, and lay back in his deckchair in the shade of the beach umbrella with the brim of a Panama hat lowered over his eyes. Massimo Rutelli was naked except for a minuscule black swimsuit and an orange towel loosely draped over his upper back, and was lying prone on the green canvas lounger provided for sun-worshippers, his hands resting on the surface of the perfectly smooth sand. But the main difference between them was that one was dead and the other was dreaming.

The dream was one that Zen had had recurrently for many months now. He had no clear idea how long exactly. His memories of the period since *l'incidente* were as partial, confused and unreliable as those of his childhood. As for the dream, it always involved three fixed elements – a bridge, an imminent disaster, and a happy ending – but the specific properties, locations and special effects varied from version to version.

The bridge, for example, could be as small as a concrete culvert under a motorway, or a massive structure so long that neither end was visible from the middle. On one occasion it had been a wooden trestle across a fast-flowing river. A steam locomotive pulling a train was approaching the far side while the ignited fuse fizzed down through the undergrowth towards the stacked sticks of dynamite. But it had been lit too late, and the carriages crossed safely before the trestles were flung spectacularly up into the air, to fall again like so many matchsticks.

Another instance had been a rope footbridge suspended across an abyss whose depths were concealed by thick, slowly coiling currents of mist. In this case the threat had come in the form of a plague of shiny black beetles nibbling away at the ropes with their razor-sharp mandibles. It was only when the last strand seemed about to give way that it became apparent that the guy lines were not made of hemp but steel cable, against which the horde of insects was powerless.

This time, though, the ever-resourceful dream director had come up with yet another scenario. Since the 1960s, there had been talk of building a bridge across the Straits of Messina to replace the slow and inadequate ferry services which provided the only link between Sicily and the mainland. At over three kilometres, it would be one of the longest in the world if ever completed, but it was not so much the engineering and construction problems which had stymied the project thus far as the economic and political ones.

The estimated cost was so vast that it was commonly expressed in dollars – $4.5 billion was one suggested figure – since the corresponding amount in lire was of an order comprehensible only to astrophysicists. During the long decades when the Christian Democrats had ruled the country, no one had had any doubt into whose hands that money would go, not to mention the inevitable cost overruns and top-ups for unforeseen circumstances which would probably at least double the original estimate. Unfinished motorways, power plants built on hastily drained swamps and steel mills erected hundreds of kilometres from the nearest source of iron ore had been a commonplace at that period, but even the most brazen politicians backed off from the prospect of being seen to hand their friends and supporters the best part of one per cent of the country's GNP. And so the bridge had never been built.

But in Aurelio Zen's dream it had, and he was in the middle of it, speeding away from Sicily, back to the safety of the mainland. The bridge itself was not the graceful suspension span which the real-life engineers had designed, but a rusty old wrought-iron girder affair originally designed to carry a railway track, now fitted out with a makeshift roadway in the

4

form of wooden planks. The car Zen was riding in was also a period piece, a huge pre-war convertible with bulgy cartoonish curves driven by a grim-looking uniformed chauffeur wearing aviator goggles. 'This is a dangerous road,' he muttered melodramatically. Zen took no notice. He was enjoying the bright sunlight, the invigorating breeze, the faint cries of the itinerant watermelon vendors on some distant beach.

They were going so fast that when the gaping hole in the planking appeared dead ahead they were almost on top of it. There was no time to brake, so the driver accelerated and the car leapt the gap, landing on the very edge of the further side, its rear wheels dangling over the void. Zen and the driver scrambled out just as the vehicle tilted back and slid off the edge of the planking. It was only now that Zen realized that there had been a third person in the car all along, a young man sitting in the back seat. He was neatly dressed in a suit and tie and seemed perfectly calm. The only odd detail was that his chest and feet were bare.

But Zen had no time to think about this, for no sooner had the car disappeared than other cracks and cavities began to open up in the surface of the bridge. It had been designed to withstand an earthquake stronger than the one that had levelled Messina in 1908, but this one must have been stronger still. Whole sections went tumbling down into the water far below, until the only one remaining was the short length where Zen was perched, and it too was now growling and shuddering beneath his feet. But the cardinal rule of these dreams was that the hero always emerged unscathed, and at this point the director – clearly out of ideas about how to save him this time – brought the episode to an abrupt end. The screen went blank as Aurelio Zen woke up.

He raised the brim of his hat and looked about him. Everything was as it always was, of course. That was the charm of Versilia, the most essential of the many elements which drew people back there year after year. There were never any surprises. Nothing unpredictable ever happened. That's what Franco's clients wanted. They weren't interested in the new, the exotic, the strange or the different. What they wanted was exactly the same as they'd been getting there for years, if not decades, and in some cases even generations. That was how long it could take to get a front row seat at the *bagno*. They were as sought after as their equivalent at La Scala, where many of Franco's patrons were regulars during the winter. Zen's allotted place was about a third of the way back from the water's edge, and he had only been able to get that because the rights in it belonged to a friend of various parties with a professional interest in keeping Zen alive and out of sight until they needed him. Without their pull, he wouldn't have been able to get a place right outside the toilets.

Not that he'd been able to hang on to it for long, he thought bitterly, glancing to his left. The man was still there, arrogantly sprawled out face down on the lounger that was rightfully Zen's, the minimalistic swimsuit displaying his massive buttocks to rather too good advantage. Zen was pleased to note that the lower half of the man's body was fully exposed to the sun now, and a nasty reddish burn was already beginning to set in on the pale skin of his legs. Serve the bastard right, he thought, moving his own chair a little further back into the deepest shade. Although the rigidly hierarchical pecking order of the beach meant nothing to him, he had become enough of a regular by now to feel abstractly affronted at this unexpected and unwelcome irregularity. The whole point of Versilia was that such things were not supposed to happen there.

The scene before him looked as flat and notional as a theatrical backdrop, two dimensions passing uneasily for three. Above, the azure sky, streaked with diaphanous shreds of white haze. Below this vast benignity, the clustered *ombrelloni*, their bright primary colours an ensign declaring the ownership of each strip of beach. The ones in the foreground were all green, as were the chairs and loungers, but behind them came serried ranks of red, yellow, blue in various shades. The white poles beneath acted as the only vertical element in the scene, breaking the seemingly endless stretch of beach into manageable rooms and apartments lacking only walls and a ceiling.

Horizontally, the divisions were still more strongly marked. Each bathing establishment had an internal passageway in the

6

form of a boardwalk bisecting its allotment. There were two rows of *ombrelloni* on either side, each centred on its own parasol positioned exactly two and a half metres from its neighbours. At the end of the boardwalk, below the high tide line, was the sea, but no one except the children paid much attention to that. The sea was merely a necessary pretext for everything else: the sensual languor, the total indolence, the studied informality of manners, the varying degrees of nudity on display. If anything, the sand – immaculately cleaned, smoothed and groomed each morning by Franco and his two sons – was the more palpable attraction. Soaking up the sun each day, until by lunchtime a pair of sandals became a necessity for those with sensitive soles, then radiating it back through the late afternoon and early evening, the dense expanse of tan granules responded to the serene sky above, the precession of the shadows cast by the parasols marking the progress of another flawless, utterly predictable day at the beach.

There were people in view too, of course. Indeed, the *bagno* was surprisingly full for a weekday. But Zen was an outsider to all the complex and overlapping cliques, circles and extended families, so for him the human element was of less interest and importance than the setting, mere extras dotted about as part of the background. They were mostly female and mostly middle-aged, although there were more than a few younger mothers and their children. What men there were had a decidedly supernumerary air about them, and tended to sit slightly apart from the rest of the family. To Zen's right, near the top end of the beach, a young couple chatted in a desultory way while the girl painstakingly squeezed out the pustules on her boyfriend's back, but most people their age were either at work or further down the beach at Viareggio, where the action was. The majority of the bikinis in Versilia were being worn by women who didn't seem to realize or care that they had reached a point in life when any men around were more likely to be mentally dressing them than the reverse.

The exception was Gemma, if that was indeed her name. There was no reason to suppose that it wasn't, but ever since *l'incidente* Zen had been living in a world where people's names, assuming they bothered to offer one, were at best generic flags of convenience, polite formulae designed to ease social contacts, of no significance or substance in themselves.

But of course Gemma belonged not to that world but to the real one whose outline Zen could vaguely make out, ever clearer but still distant, from the middle of the bridge he was slowly and painfully traversing, hour by hour, day by day, week after week. One of the most delightful things about Gemma was that she knew nothing of all that. Apart from shopkeepers and taxi drivers, she was the only person Zen had come into contact with since the 'incident' who didn't know. This had lent an extra charm and interest to their brief and superficial encounters. Zen was using her, he realized, as a test case, looking anxiously to see if he could once again pass for normal. The results, so far, had been encouraging.

He had checked on Gemma as soon as he awakened. There had, of course, been no need. Like everyone else on the beach, with the exception of the pushy newcomer to Zen's left, she was exactly where she ought to be, exactly where he'd known she would be: stretched out on her own canvas lounger, her long delicate feet dangling over the end, the right one twitching from time to time like the tail of a cow bothered by flies. Her face was turned away from him, but he knew she wasn't sleeping. She was napping, a very different matter. They had once had a mock-earnest argument about this fine distinction, as near as they had so far come to moving beyond the strictly conventional.

Gemma had the *ombrellone* directly opposite Zen's, which made it possible for them to acknowledge each other's existence. Social life at Franco's was rigidly hierarchical. Those in the front rows, the old aristocracy of the establishment, 'knew' only each other, although they might occasionally so far unbend as to grant a nod and a word to a friend or close acquaintance – possibly even a superior in the world left behind where the sand began – who was stacked further back, in the faceless ranks of parvenus and hoi polloi. But in general casual fraternization was permitted only with those seated immediately to one side or facing your own designated place. This had made it possible for Gemma and Zen to exchange glances, nods and eventually greetings; the fact that they were much of an age, and apparently unattached, had made it inevitable. Once it had been established that they both avoided the beach when the weekend crowds descended, a sort of light, meaningless connection formed.

After a while Gemma started to stir, and then sat up lazily, looking around her. She was a slim, leggy, small-breasted woman, and surprisingly tall. She noticed Zen watching her, but didn't wave or smile. Instead she folded up the magazine she'd been reading, found the linen bag in which she kept her beach paraphernalia, put on her rubber sandals and then walked over the wooden pathway to where he was sitting.

'Signor Pier Giorgio,' she said. 'You're awake.'

Zen gave a self-deprecatory grimace.

'Just pretending,' he said.

Gemma tilted her eyes and head towards the intruder who had taken Zen's place and gestured interrogatively. Zen signed back that he didn't have a clue.

'I was just going to get a coffee,' Gemma said. 'Would you like one?'

'That's very kind.'

'Espresso?'

'Please.'

Gemma turned without a word or gesture and walked up the beach towards the low shack in whose shaded bar Franco dispensed coffee, soft drinks, beer, light snacks and ice cream. I wonder if she can sew, Zen thought. Since his mother had died, his clothes were falling to pieces. He could always take them to a seamstress, of course, but paying for that kind of work seemed like paying for sex. It took all the goodness out of it.

He caught himself up with a shock. This was all too typical of the free-flowing, dreamlike way his brain was working these days. Whatever happened between him and Gemma, it would never be anything more than the classic beach romance, he reminded himself sternly, at whatever level from flirting to fornication. Nothing more. He had to start thinking straight again. He needed to get back to life, back to work. But there was nothing he could do about that. He was trapped in limbo, midway across the bridge, neither here nor there. He closed his eyes again.

The next thing he was aware of was a woman's cry. Gemma was standing about halfway between her place and the complex of changing rooms, showers and bar area. She held a coffee cup in each hand, and was staring down at her lower body. Behind her, a young man wearing a T-shirt and jeans was running off at full tilt towards the street. Zen got to his feet, but Gemma was already surrounded by other people who had been seated closer to her. He could hear the excited chatter of voices expressing dismay and disgust. After a few moments, Gemma brushed off the crowd of sympathizers, saying something about needing to change, and returned to the bar. Zen followed.

It was blissfully cool and shady under the roof of straw matting supported on wires above the bar area. Gemma was nowhere to be seen. Zen sidled up to the bar, where Franco acknowledged his presence with the ghost of a nod. He had accepted the arrangement that his long-time client Girolamo Rutelli had imposed, and allowed this stranger access to the facilities rented annually by the family for as long as anyone could remember, but he made a point of reminding Zen that this made him no more than an honorary member of the club, the guest of a member, to be accommodated correctly but without undue warmth.

If Zen had been a bit more forthcoming about his own circumstances, this might have changed, but he had no such inclination. His cover story was paper-thin, and depended for its success on no one taking the trouble to check it at all carefully. Franco's role in life, Zen had already realized, apart from milking the summer trade for all its three months' life was worth, was to act as the catchment area, filter and conduit for any local gossip worth knowing. Radio Franco was always on the air, and if Zen had allowed himself to be quizzed about the vague and unsupported fictions he had been provided with, he would have been exposed for the fraud he was in no time at all. On the other hand, refusing to reply to Franco's seemingly casual questions would have been equally inadvisable. Zen's strategy had been to keep his distance, treating Franco not as the universal uncle he aspired to be but simply as the owner of the *bagno*, a paid service provider of no personal interest whatever.

He seated himself at one of the metal tables in the bar area, but did not order anything. After a few minutes, Gemma emerged from her changing room, wearing her street clothes. Their eyes met, and Zen beckoned her over.

'What happened?' he asked.

Gemma tossed her head.

'Oh, just a stupid accident. I was on my way back with the coffee, when this young idiot barged into me and knocked it all over me. It was quite painful, and it stained my suit of course. I've washed it out, but I hate wearing wet clothes so I'm going to go home.'

'Was he the one who ran off?'

'Who? Oh, yes. The funny thing is he was standing there staring at you.'

'At me?'

'Yes. You were sitting there with your eyes closed, and this kid was standing on the boardwalk staring at you, as if you were some kind of star or something. Then he suddenly whirled round and ran straight into me with the coffee.'

The word seemed to jolt Zen's memory. He looked up at the bar and directed the owner to bring them two coffees. The owner scowled and yelled inside for his wife.

'What did he look like, this man?' Zen asked Gemma.

She shrugged.

'Like anyone else that age.'

'What age?'

'About thirty, I suppose.'

'You don't remember anything else about him?'

'I only saw him for an instant. After that I was covered in scalding coffee and had other things to think about.'

She reflected for a moment.

'He had something written on his shirt,' she said at last.

'What?'

'I don't remember. Some slogan in English. What does it matter?'

Franco's wife brought their coffees. Zen smiled.

'It doesn't, as long as you're all right. It's just odd, that's all. Nothing unusual ever happens here, and this is the second case today.'

'What's the first?'

'That man who's taken my place.'

Gemma nodded.

'You should have called Franco, had him moved.'

'I didn't want to make a scene. What's the point? The Brunellis never come during the week anyway, so I just took their spot.'

Gemma finished her coffee.

'Well, I'll be going,' she said.

Zen stood up as she did.

'I don't suppose you'd like to have dinner tonight,' he found himself saying.

She regarded him intensely.

'Dinner? But why?'

He gestured embarrassedly.

'Why not?'

This seemed to give her pause.

'Why not?' she repeated at length.

'Good. About eight at Augusto's. Do you know it?'

'Of course, everyone knows it. Have you made a booking?'

Zen shook his head.

'Then we'll never get in,' Gemma said decisively. 'They're booked up weeks in advance.'

'I can get us a table. Trust me.'

Gemma looked at him again in that odd, intense way of hers.

'Very well,' she said. 'I'll trust you.'

She gave him a vague smile and walked off down the pathway at the side of the building leading to the car park. Zen headed back to the beach.

He noticed the police at once. There were three of them, two men and a woman, all young and looking very sporty in the starched sky-blue shorts and summer shirts of the municipal police. They were stretched out evenly across the beach from the tideline to the land end, walking slowly and checking everything and everyone in their range.

By the time Zen got back to his place, the female officer had just reached Franco's boardwalk. Zen went over to her.

'Excuse me,' he said with a pleasant smile backed up by a hint of the steely sheen of power. 'I'm in the police myself, down in Rome. Criminalpol. Is anything wrong?'

The woman gave him the merest glance and shook her head.

'Routine patrol,' she said. 'But we had some reports of someone passing as an itinerant trader, a *vucumprà*. Did you see anyone like that?'

'How do you mean, "passing"?'

'When he raised his sleeve, his skin was white from the elbow. And he didn't look African. That's what we were told, anyway.'

'I can't imagine any outsider wanting to cut a piece of that market,' Zen remarked.

'No, but he might have had other things in mind. People trust the Moroccans. Well, most of them are Sudanese actually, but the point is that they police themselves very effectively. They make a sale or they don't, but no one gets ripped off. Same with the Chinese masseurs and fortune tellers. But there have been several robberies reported on the beach recently, people's handbags and cameras disappearing while they're away from their place, and if some white person has made himself up to look like the immigrants, he might get away with it. There are plenty of Albanians and gypsies about, and they can be very imaginative. Normally they do houses, sometimes while the owners are asleep, but this might be a new angle.'

She looked at her two companions, who had drawn ahead, and nodded goodbye to Zen. He picked up his scattered belongings and started pensively back. That was the third anomaly this afternoon, he thought. First the stranger taking his place, then the young man who had stared at him and then rammed into Gemma, and now somebody impersonating one of the African traders. Anywhere else, this would have been a very average day's haul of minor mysteries, but in the placid, predictable world of the beach it was a potential front-page news story. Perhaps there's a pattern, thought Zen, smiling sourly at his wishful thinking.

This enforced vacation was driving him slightly crazy, he realized. What he needed was to get back to work, but there was no prospect of that. The powers that be had their plans for him, and it had been made gently clear to him that these included an early and well-deserved retirement. 'We'll have to bend the rules,' one of the official visitants to his hospital bed had told him. 'But it's the least you deserve after all you've been through.'

He walked back past the bar, nodding to Franco and getting a grudging raise of the chin in return, and out into the full glare of the sun. As always, he was surprised to see the line of craggy mountains dominating the skyline to the east, their gleaming white surfaces making them seem even higher than they were in the July heat, although their lustre was not, of course, snow but marble.

He crunched across the gravel parking lot and crossed the *lungomare* which ran all the way from Carrara to Viareggio, almost thirty kilometres in all, connecting the various villages and fishing ports which had now turned into a continuous strip of coastal development, retaining only their names and some vestiges of their original centres. Few of the buildings were more than a hundred years old, and the vast majority less than half that. Until the beach craze set in after the war, these marshy lowlands had been home to only a few stately villas set amidst the ribbon of wild pines which had once fringed the sea all the way south to Rome.

The main road was impressively broad, but the virtual absence of traffic gave it the same slightly unreal feel as the rest of the area. This was even more marked in the back streets beyond, which motorized vehicles entered strictly on sufferance, and at a crawl. The narrow lanes were filled with pedestrians and cyclists wandering about without so much as a cautious glance to check what was coming. Everything was clean, neat and safe, a privileged enclave where the normal chaos theory of Italian urban life was inverted. Zen had initially found it charming, just what he needed in his prolonged convalescence, but now it was starting to grate on him. There was no edge, no friction, no coefficient of resistance. There were moments when he had to curb the urge to start behaving badly, just to stir things up a little.

But that would not have done, any more than it would have done not to visit the beach every day. The truth was that Zen much preferred to avoid the sun, if at all possible, and also hated sitting still doing nothing for hours on end. But his instructions were to blend in, and to come to Versilia and not go to the beach would have made him an exception to the prevailing rule and thereby an object of interest and comment. So he put in his four or five hours a day, like going to the office, and then walked sedately home, resisting the impulse to bump into people, utter insulting innuendoes and make sarcastic remarks. It was a strain, but he had his orders.

Nor could he leave. His orders on this point too were clear. He was to remain exactly where he was until contacted. Besides, he had nowhere else to go. He had not returned to Rome since the death of his mother, and felt no desire to do so. To attempt another false return to Venice was even more out of the question. The mere thought of either alternative made him realize how cluttered with the past his life had become, how devoid of any viable future. This was still more depressing, and seemingly insoluble, so he tried to think of other things, or better still not to think at all. That was all he needed to do, he told himself for the umpteenth time, just stop thinking and enjoy this pleasant, calm, mindless existence that most people could only dream of. What was the matter with him? Why was nothing ever good enough?

He dropped in to the small *alimentari* where he did his daily shopping. His invitation to Gemma had been only partly motivated by a wish to know her better. The fact was that ever since his arrival he had been living off whatever cooked dishes the place had on offer that day, or those he could forage and prepare for himself, a very limited cuisine consisting largely of packet soups, frozen entrées, sandwiches and takeaway pizza. To dine out alone would be another anomaly of the kind he was not permitted by the terms of his contract. Even shopping alone, as a middle-aged male, was anomalous, but he had to eat.

He stocked up on coffee, milk, bread and a few eggs. The cashier looked at him in the same way that Franco did, as though she was confused by recognizing yet not being able to place him. That look, in another pair of eyes, could yet get him killed, he thought idly. The fact was that he didn't really care. The Mafia might not have killed him physically, but something in him had died, something without which life didn't really seem worth the effort. He just didn't care about anything, that was the real and lasting effect of *l'incidente*, and one which looked as though it might well stay with him throughout his long, tedious, enforced retirement, a nagging ache that no amount of therapy, exercise or hobbies would ever be able to dispel.

Opposite the grocery, from a white lorry parked at the kerb, fresh vegetables, fruit and eggs were being sold to a bevy of housewives, all of whom were giving the vendor a hard time about his quality, selection and prices, a daily ritual necessary to everyone's sense of dignity and self-esteem. The women knew that short of driving to one of the supermarkets on the highway inland, they were stuck with what Mario had on offer, in very much the same way that they were stuck with their husbands, children, relatives, homes and general lot in life. Their only perk was the right to bitch loudly and at length about the inequities of the situation, and in this they indulged freely. Mario, understanding that this was one of the costs of doing business, entered into the ensuing series of mini-dramas with gusto and vivacity, playing his part to the full.

Zen drifted back across to the shady side of the street, taking in the scene at the greengrocer's van, a cluster of young people on bicycles, a group of women cooing over a neighbour's baby, a man leaning against a concrete telephone pole eating an ice cream and eyeing the passers-by. He was wearing a T-shirt with some sort of English slogan on it. Zen walked down two blocks to the end of the commercial area, then turned left into a street old enough to pre-date the rigid grid which had been imposed on later development, curving gently off past wrought-iron gates and spurts of greenery spilling over weathered walls. The villa which he had been assigned was about halfway along the curve, which ended at a crumbling gateway leading into one of the last remaining portions of the original *pineta*. There was virtually no traffic at all, and no sound to disturb the silence but the perpetual murmur of televisions and the occasional yapping of a small, neurotic dog kept by one of the neighbours.

He reached his gate, and for some reason paused before unlocking it to glance over his shoulder. There was no one in sight. *So they already know where you live,* said a voice in his head. 'Oh, shut up!' Zen muttered audibly. Such professional paranoia was like the vanity of one of those women on the beach who couldn't get used to the fact that the sexual stock she had been living off for the last thirty years had just tanked in the market. 'We're both yesterday's men,' he had told Don Gaspare Limina in Sicily, and he had been right. Why couldn't he accept that he was no longer a player, and never would be again? In the event the Mafia had failed to kill him, thanks to a stroke of luck and their own incompetence, but he was as good as dead just the same.

The gravel driveway inside the gate led to a stairway at the side of the house. At first-floor level this connected with a balcony running along the west face. Zen passed the shuttered windows and unlocked the door giving access to his domain. He took his groceries through to the kitchen immediately to the left of the front door and put them away neatly, then returned to the large *salotto* which took up most of the apartment and slumped down in an armchair, wincing slightly. The panoply of pain that he had lived with for so long had now lifted, but there were still a few malcontent twinges and jabs prepared to make his life a misery if he stretched too far in the wrong direction, or went to sleep in an unsuitable position, or generally overexerted himself in almost any way whatever. The doctors he went to consult once a week at the hospital in

Pietrasanta had assured him that there was no permanent damage, and that any 'perceived discomfort' was purely superficial, temporary and nothing to worry about. He believed them, but these pains were less like the dramatic and evidently causal agony he had suffered in the months immediately following the explosion than the normal discomforts of age and decrepitude, telltale signs that the body was reaching the end of its useful life. This somehow made them even less bearable.

He closed his eyes, feeling the delicious cool of the high-ceilinged room begin to massage his stress away. How many such rooms had he passed through on the long journey back to his present convalescence? He would never know. Of the first few weeks, his mind retained only jagged little splinters of memory, precise yet totally specific and uncontextualized. For the rest, he had to rely on what he'd been told. The driver had hauled him out of the burning car and radioed for help, and they'd both been rushed to hospital in Catania. After the immediate operation for a collapsed lung, Zen had been transferred by air to a military hospital on the island of Santo Stefano, off the Sardinian coast, where he had spent weeks in traction. Later he had been moved again, first to a sanatorium in the Adige valley, then to a private nursing home in the hills above Genoa.

In all that time, he had seen no one that he knew or could trust, except in the impersonal sense in which you trust a garage mechanic to repair your car. His body had had the best of attention, but it was only gradually that he had come to understand that the reason why the authorities were lavishing such care on him was because they needed him alive and presentable to testify at an upcoming trial in the United States. The most informative and forthcoming of his visitors had been a young man from the Ministry of Foreign Affairs, who had managed to intimate, without of course naming any names, that the Americans had succeeded in arresting a number of prominent mafiosi who had been on the Italian 'most wanted' list for years, including two members of the Ragusa clan whom Zen had identified from photographs in the course of a preliminary debriefing at the military base on Santo Stefano. This tended to reflect rather poorly on the Italian authorities, the young diplomat had continued, and it was unanimously felt at the highest levels that to send a hero of the unceasing domestic struggle against 'the octopus' to the USA, to testify in person that he had seen Nello and Giulio Rizzo unloading illegal drugs from the plane on which he himself had just arrived from Malta, would help redress the balance and generally help the home side cut a better international *figura*.

Meanwhile, all he had to do was wait and make the most of the amenities of the accommodation that had been placed at his disposal. Which, he had to admit, were considerable. The property was apparently owned by two brothers named Rutelli, one based in Turin and the other in Rome, who divided it between them for vacation use. Zen had been allotted the upper storey, while the lower one had been empty until the day before, when he had heard noises indicating that someone had moved in. This someone was presumably the other brother, but Zen had been given no instructions to make contact with him, and had not done so.

The floor he had was more than ample for his needs. There were two bedrooms, a pleasant bathroom, the small but adequate kitchen, and this great living area which breathed an air of calmer, more spacious times. Zen had always believed that every building came with its own aura, a sort of immaterial scent you picked up the moment you crossed the threshold. But unlike a scent, this couldn't be sprayed on. It was unique and inalienable, and told the sensitive visitor much about the people who had lived in the space and the things that had happened there. Zen had been in beautiful houses he could hardly wait to get out of, so overwhelmingly oppressive was the sense of evil and despair which they radiated, and also in fetid inner-city tenements that felt as serene as a monastery cell. This room was visually pleasing, in a restrained, craftsmanlike way, but its real gift to him was the overwhelming sense of peace and contentment it radiated. He didn't know who had lived there, but he would have testified under oath to their moral character and general probity.

That was his last thought until he woke to find the room significantly darker and the clock showing twenty minutes past seven. It took him another moment to remember his dinner date with Gemma, for which he still had not made a booking. He had boastfully said that he could get them into Augusto's, counting on using Girolamo Rutelli's name to do the trick, but he hadn't counted on leaving it this late.

In the event, this proved to be no problem. He had only just dialled the number of the restaurant when the phone was answered by an obsequious voice saying, 'Augusto's. Good evening, Dottor Rutelli.'

Zen was speechless for a moment. Then he said, 'How did you know it was me?'

'We have Caller Identification installed, *dottore*. I explained it to you last time, don't you remember? That way we can filter out the riff-raff and answer only the calls that matter. What can we do for you?'

'I'd like a table for two this evening. About eight, if that's possible.'

'*Ma certo, dottore. Come no? Alle otto. Benissimo. Al piacere di rivederla.*'

'I'll be dining with a friend named Pier Giorgio Butani,' Zen went on. 'If I'm a little late, please look after him.'

He took a shower and then carefully picked out some suitable clothing in the casually formal mode which was the evening norm in Versilia. Realizing that this was a tricky balance to bring off successfully, Zen had taken the bus to Viareggio shortly after his arrival and put himself in the hands of one of the men's outfitters there. As always, his aim was to remain invisible. 'Get lost in the crowd,' the young man from the Farnesina had told him. 'Keep your head down, melt into the background, don't draw attention to yourself. We have decided against providing you with a resident bodyguard for that very reason, although there will be people keeping an eye on you. But Versilia's full of tourists at this time of year, and as long as you're reasonably cautious there's no earthly reason why anyone should give you a second thought. Just remember who you're supposed to be, and try to look the part.' This last was a reference to one Pier Giorgio Butani, a distant cousin of Girolamo Rutelli. Butani really existed, just in case anyone checked, but he had moved with his parents to Argentina in the mid-Fifties, only rarely visited Italy and had never been to Versilia.

Zen left the house at a quarter to eight, which gave him just enough time to reach the restaurant in time by cutting across the park at the end of the street. The sun was already down behind the umbrella pines, the air was fresh but still pleasantly warm. The birds that flocked in the gardens all around were chirping and chattering loudly, but there was no other sound. Zen passed under the gateway to the original estate, past the ruins of the porter's lodge, and over a hump bridge across one of the narrow canals constructed a century or more earlier to drain the malarial swamps.

In the wood, the shadows were gathering swiftly. The birds here were larger and louder, rarely showing themselves except to swoop in packs across the track in front. To either side, the undergrowth was dense and impenetrable, except to the various small animals which could be heard scuttling away at the sound or smell of this intruder.

It was only when he turned left on to the track leading back towards the shoreline that Zen noticed the other man. He was about thirty metres back, walking calmly along. By now it was almost dark beneath the tall pines. Zen could just make out that the man seemed to be wearing jeans and a short jacket of some kind, and was glancing about him to either side as though admiring the beauties of nature.

Zen ignored the warning signal which automatically sounded in his brain, and carried on towards the invisible strip of streets where Augusto's was situated. He had to learn to become an ordinary civilian again, he told himself. The days of danger and glory were over. No one was trying to kill him, no one was even interested in his existence except as a token witness at a foreign trial, flown in like a consignment of truffles or rare wine, a luxury import to impress the locals and make the old country look good. Nevertheless, he counted off another thirty metres, and then dropped his bunch of keys. Retrieving them, he noted that the other walker had also made a left turn at the parting of the ways.

For a moment, he was half inclined to force a confrontation and find out who the man was, but then it occurred to him that it might well be one of those whom he'd been told would be 'keeping an eye on him'. If so, that would be unprofessional and an embarrassment for all concerned. And if not, it would break the cardinal rule of his existence here in Versilia, which was not to draw attention to himself. In the end he decided to do nothing, but he lengthened his stride as much as possible, eager to see the bright lights and crowded streets again.

He was looking forward to his dinner with Gemma, even though he knew hardly anything about her. In the long wearisome months since the 'incident' and the death of his mother, he had been alone almost the whole time, apart of course from the purely professional and usually painful attentions of doctors, nurses, policemen and bureaucrats. However the evening turned out, it would be a welcome change from all that. And if he knew nothing about Gemma, she knew even less about him. Almost everything he'd told her during their very brief exchanges had necessarily been a lie. He reminded himself that he was going to have to keep that up during the whole of the time they were together, adding new details where called for, but such as were consistent with what Gemma already knew. Maybe it wasn't going to be such a relaxing evening after all.

At last the gateway at the south-western edge of the former estate appeared in the gloom up ahead. This time, Zen risked an unmotivated glance behind. The man who had been there was nowhere to be seen, but they had passed many minor paths off through the undergrowth to either side, any one of which he might have taken. A moment later Zen had crossed another of the drainage canals, and was out in the streets leading down to the sea.

Da Augusto, as its folksy name suggested, looked like a perfectly ordinary fish restaurant anywhere from one end of the Versilia resort coastline to the other. It consisted of a nondescript two-storey building on a back street three blocks inland from the *lungomare*, with a glass extension jutting out to the kerb at the front and a garden area with a retractable awning at the rear. There was nothing to suggest that it was anything other than a reasonably decent eatery serving reasonably fresh fish cooked reasonably well at a more or less reasonable price. It was only when you tried to get a table that it became apparent that there was rather more to it than that.

The distinction was based not so much on the food, which was at best a notch or so above many other places in the area, as on the restaurant's unchallenged pedigree as the chosen haunt of almost every Italian political and show business personality of the last half century, many of whose personally inscribed photographs lined the walls. What had happened off camera was reputedly still more interesting. That table in the corner, according to some, was where Anita Ekberg was being entertained by Marcello Mastroianni on the memorable evening when she bent down to retrieve something from her handbag, causing her unsupported right breast to tumble out of her dress. According to others, that one over there, against the wall, was where Giulio Andreotti and a group of his closest allies had decided not to negotiate with the Red Brigades to secure the release of Aldo Moro. And over there, at the back of the main room, rumour had it that a groupie had crawled under the table and brought a certain pop star to orgasm in her mouth on a bet from another member of the band, who wanted to see if she could make the star in question bring the events in progress to the attention of the staff and customers. She had reputedly succeeded.

Zen was greeted by a functionary who managed to combine the glacial serenity of the traditional English butler with the menacing directness of a Mafia thug. His first glance at Zen amply revealed the extent to which he was unimpressed by this new arrival.

'My name is Pier Giorgio Butani,' Zen told him in a tone suggesting that he was even less impressed. 'I am dining with Dottor Rutelli.'

For a moment, the functionary's composure deserted him completely.

'Dottor Rutelli?' he whispered. 'But he's . . .'

Already here, thought Zen glumly. Damn. The doorman was staring at Zen with something approaching desperation.

'Massimo Rutelli?' he queried at length.

Zen shook his head tetchily.

'What? No! His brother, Girolamo.'

The man laughed almost hysterically. He grabbed a leather-bound menu.

'Ah, yes, of course! Right! This way, please. Just over here. Be so good as to take a seat. May I take your coat? Thank you, thank you.'

Zen sat down, took out his mobile phone and loudly faked a call.

'Girolamo?' he shouted, glancing idly at the menu. 'Oh, where the hell are you? I'm starving. Me? At Augusto's, of course. What? What? Why? Really? Oh, too bad! Well, so be it. I'll call you tomorrow, okay? All right. Fine, fine.'

Just as he replaced the phone, a stunningly beautiful woman walked into the restaurant and stood looking around quizzically. It took Zen a moment to recognize her. He'd almost never seen her fully clothed before, he realized, pushing back his chair and hurrying over.

'Gemma, my dear! What a surprise! And what a great pleasure. Now you haven't eaten, have you? And what were your plans?'

He turned her away towards the wall and pretended to listen, nodding sympathetically while she explained her plans. In reality, Gemma was staring at him with an expression which mingled amusement and alarm.

'Oh no you're not!' Zen declared decisively, taking her arm and steering her into the room. 'Wasting your time with those boring little people? Out of the question! You're dining with me, my dear, and that's that.'

He paused to confront the doorman.

'I just phoned Dottor Rutelli. Unfortunately he's been forced to cancel our dinner engagement due to urgent personal problems, but he was kind enough to invite me to use the booking on my own behalf. He specially recommended the *lasagnette con pesce cappone*. We'll have that as a starter.'

24

He ushered Gemma, who was by now almost giggling, over to the table.

'What on earth was that all about?' she demanded, taking off her cream linen jacket and hanging it on the back of the chair.

'Don't complain. I told you I'd get us a reservation, and I have.'

'So you know the Rutelli brothers. Of course, I should have realized, that's who normally has that *tavolo* where you are now.'

'I don't really know them. Girolamo is the friend of a friend. But I knew he had a house here which he wouldn't be using until August, so I arranged to borrow it for a few weeks. The friend owes me a favour and Rutelli owes him one. The old story.'

'I only know them by sight myself. We nod and greet each other, of course, but to tell the truth I've never really managed to tell them apart. Rather ordinary little men, I always thought.'

'Well, they have their uses. Apparently the staff here don't know that at the moment Girolamo's in Rome, so I used his name to get a booking. After that it was just a matter of faking a previous engagement for our supposed host and the table is ours.'

Gemma laughed and shook her head.

'Well, at least you're not boring,' she said. 'I didn't realize you were so well connected locally.'

'I'm not at all. In fact I don't know a soul here except you.'

Always tell as much of the truth as possible, he reminded himself. Most liars got caught out unnecessarily falsifying or embroidering quite trivial details.

'And what about you?' he asked, gazing at her.

She was wearing an apricot-coloured short-sleeved blouse of what looked like coarse silk, open at the neck to reveal a flat gold chain at her tanned throat. Her auburn-tinged hair had clearly been redone since leaving the beach, and her finger-nails were painted a bright orange to match her blouse and lip-stick. She's dolled herself up, thought Zen, using a vulgar Venetian dialect expression. Then he realized that she would naturally have done so, not wanting to look out of place at

Augusto's. There was no reason to assume that it had anything to do with him.

'Oh, I'm just a day tripper,' Gemma replied. 'I actually live in Lucca, so it's easy enough to get here and back.'

'Is it close?'

'Half an hour on the *bretella*. Quick enough to come back for dinner. Have you been there?'

Zen was once again glad to be able to answer truthfully.

'Never.'

The waiter arrived with a bottle of the house white and a platter of *insalata di mare*. Another of the many traditions of Augusto's was that if you were too preoccupied to order, as so many important clients naturally tended to be, dishes just arrived at the table.

'It's a dull little city,' Gemma went on, 'but very calm.'

'Is your family there?'

'My father lives close by, in a nursing home. My brothers and sisters have all moved away. I did myself, once, but I came back.'

'So you live alone?'

Gemma hesitated.

'Except when my son comes to visit,' she said.

Zen nibbled some marinated squid.

'How old is he?'

'Twenty. He's studying engineering in Florence. That's where my husband lives. Stefano stays with him. And you?'

Zen raised his head like a tennis player realizing that what he had thought to be an unreturnable volley was in fact skimming back to his side of the court.

'Me?'

'Family,' said Gemma. 'Children.'

'No,' said Zen.

Gemma laughed.

'You're parthenogenetic?'

'Sorry?'

'Yours was a virgin birth?'

'What? Oh no. My parents are both dead, and I have no children. That's all.'

Gemma blushed and looked a little flustered.

'I'm sorry, that must have sounded tactless. I must stop trying to make jokes. It never works.'

'Oh, don't do that. There's so little to laugh at as one gets older that even the intention is encouraging.'

They finished their starters and were silent for a while.

'So where do you live?' asked Gemma as the waiter came with the dish of *lasagnette.*

'In Rome,' Zen replied. 'I work for one of the ministries, in a mid-level bureaucratic position.'

'Which one?'

'Interior.'

'I thought you *statali* all got your holidays in August.'

'Well, this is not really a holiday, as such. My mother died recently. I took it quite hard – she was all I had left, really – and the Ministry granted me some compassionate leave.'

Noting Gemma's serious expression, he decided to lighten the tone.

'Come August, I'll be sweltering in my office, the one with the windows painted shut, while everyone else is at the beach or in the mountains.'

He drank some wine.

'And what about you?'

'I own a pharmacy which I inherited from my father.'

Zen smiled sourly.

'I've always thought that a permit to run a pharmacy or a tobacconist's was the next best thing to a licence to print money.'

Gemma smiled aloofly.

'Well, I don't know about that, but we do quite nicely. The location is excellent, on Via Fillungo, one of the main streets, and I employ three very bright, competent women to look after the shop. The clients trust them, rightly, and their wages reflect that. The business more or less runs itself. Apart from keeping an eye on inventory and sales, I'm not that involved these days.'

Zen smiled and nodded. He was astonished at how well the evening was going. It was because they were where they were, he supposed. In Versilia, any encounter was by definition a holiday event, with no implications for the future. If he and

Gemma had met anywhere else, and had been having dinner on such a casual basis, the whole evening would have been fraught with implied or perceived meanings, but here it was innocent. Nothing that mattered happened at the beach, and nothing that happened there mattered. It was as simple as that.

Zen had just launched into a rather amusing anecdote concerning a dentist in his native Canareggio district of Venice, when he realized firstly that Pier Giorgio Butani had not grown up in Venice, and secondly that Gemma was not listening. Or rather she was not listening to him. Her attention was completely distracted by an expansive women in her late forties who had materialized at their table. Zen vaguely remembered having seen her on the beach.

'Gemma, my dear, have you heard the news?' she cried.

'What news?'

Gemma seemed less than enchanted by this turn of events.

'Massimo Rutelli!'

'What about him?'

'You haven't heard? He's dead!'

Gemma gave a facial shrug.

'Really?'

The woman looked offended at Gemma's lack of response.

'You don't understand! He was dead all afternoon! Sitting there right beside us on the beach!'

'What do you mean?'

'He was lying on his lounger at Franco's and apparently he had a stroke or something! I saw him there with that towel stretched over his back. I thought, oh yes it's Signor Rutelli, although I didn't know which one and all the time it was a corpse lying there! It's horrible, just horrible! I feel sort of unclean, you know what I mean? That such a thing should happen here, of all places.'

'Yes, well, death can come at inconvenient times. My maternal grandfather passed away on the lavatory. He always used to spend a long time in there, and it was hours before we found him. Now that really did make us feel unclean. Never mind, it'll all be forgotten in a few days.'

She flashed the woman a cool and very final smile, and

turned back pointedly to face Zen. But the intruder was not to be put off so easily.

'Aren't you going to introduce me to your friend?' she enquired cattily. 'The mystery man! We've all been wondering who was usurping the Rutellis' place.'

Zen stood up and held out his hand.

'Pier Giorgio Butani, signora. I am Girolamo Rutelli's cousin. I knew his brother only slightly, but needless to say I'm appalled at this dreadful news.'

This too was true. Anything which brought attention to the Rutelli family risked bringing attention to Zen and thereby blowing his cover.

'Teresa Pananelli,' the woman returned with a decidedly flirtatious smile. 'I'm so glad that you at least are treating this tragedy with the proper gravity, Signor Butani. But then Gemma's always been frivolous and flippant, haven't you, my dear? We were at school together, and I remember some of the tricks she used to play on our poor teachers . . .'

Zen smiled politely. Gemma said nothing. Signora Pananelli emitted a sound rather like a hiss. She leaned forward to Zen, touching him on the sleeve.

'And it didn't end there,' she confided in a stage whisper. 'The stories I could tell! Particularly since Tommaso and she split up.'

She laughed loudly and insincerely.

'Anyway, be warned! When it comes to men, Gemma eats them up and spits them out. There was a tennis pro at the Club Nettuno who lasted almost the whole season, but normally the turnover's much faster than that. Well, I must be getting back to my friends. A pleasure to have met you, Signor Butani. Ciao, Gemma!'

Zen sat down again.

'Well, she was certainly . . .' he began.

'Don't say anything!' snapped Gemma. 'Just don't say anything.'

She was staring at the tablecloth so furiously that it seemed she might burn a hole in it. Zen signalled the waiter to take their plates.

'*Per secondo?*' the waiter queried.

'Fish,' said Zen.

'What kind?'

'The freshest.'

'All our fish are fresh,' the waiter retorted grittily.

'Then it doesn't matter which kind. Grilled, with *patate fritte* and a dish of *insalata di fagiolini verdi*. And more and better wine.'

The waiter took himself off in a huff.

'I hope you don't mind me ordering,' Zen said to Gemma.

'Why should I?'

'Some women might.'

'I'm not interested in tokenistic gestures. If I want to assert myself, you won't be in any doubt about it. Besides, your choice was perfectly correct.'

'Thank you,' Zen replied with a smidgen of irony.

'That bitch.'

'*La Pananelli?*'

'What a fucking nerve. I mean, really! She was right, we were at school together. What she didn't mention was that she left a year after I arrived.'

'She was expelled?'

An abrupt shake of the head.

'A little question of age, *caro*. And she's been on my case ever since, peeking and prying, gossiping and insinuating. I don't know what her problem is. Except I do, which just makes it worse. Thank God I only see her here at the beach.'

'What is her problem?'

'Don't try and pretend you're interested!'

Zen looked at her neutrally and said nothing.

'I'm sorry,' Gemma went on. 'She really got to me and I'm taking it out on you. I apologize.'

'That's all right.'

'Her problem is that she sees me as her vicarious double. She's too stupid to realize it, of course, but that's the situation all right. Teresa married her childhood sweetheart, a consulting engineer who knows everything there is to know about reinforced concrete. I was once at a birthday party she threw for him where he showed a selection of slides he had taken all over the world showing different types of rebar.'

'What's that?'

Gemma laughed.

'Be thankful you didn't ask Sandro that question. It's the metal gristle that holds concrete together. It comes in various shapes and forms. Each country has its preferred kind. The differences are slight but extraordinarily significant.'

'I get the picture.'

Their main course arrived, a succulent mullet grilled to perfection.

'But Sandro's own rebar seems to have rusted out, judging by various remarks which Teresa let drop in an attempt to get me interested in her affairs. Not that I needed her to tell me. Look at her, sitting over there. Go ahead, stare! Christ knows she and her pals are staring at us. Note the tremulous, pouting lower lip? A sure sign of the unfucked. Sad but true.'

She drank some wine as though to quench her thirst.

'Forgive me being so frank. I would have preferred to have carried on with the civilized evening we were having, but since Teresa made those comments about me, I thought I'd better try and put them in perspective.'

Zen noted that although Gemma had explained why her nemesis had made the allegations about her, she hadn't attempted to deny them.

'Anyway, at least we know who took my place at the beach and why,' he replied brightly. 'He paid a stiff price, the poor bastard.'

He grinned at Gemma.

'And now let's change the subject, and try and at least pretend to be enjoying ourselves. After all, if that woman was trying to ruin your evening, we don't want to give her the satisfaction of thinking that she's succeeded.'

Gemma grinned back.

'I like the way you think. God this fish is good! They've done nothing to it, just a hint of coriander and fennel. And have you tried the potatoes? Light as a feather.'

'All right, all right, don't overdo it.'

'So where are you from?'

'Venice,' he answered without thinking.

'Really? But no one's from Venice any more.'

'I am that no one.'

'That explains why we're both so stubborn. Lucca's the only city in Tuscany that was never conquered by the Florentines, and Venice was never conquered by anyone.'

'Until the end.'

'Yes, and when it happened we both chose a championship conqueror in Napoleon, who handed both cities over to his uninspiring but well-intentioned Habsburg in-laws. Not a bad way to finish up, when you look at the alternatives.'

She pushed her plate aside.

'Now let's get out of here.'

'No dessert, coffee, nothing?'

'There's a good *gelateria* just up the road, near where I parked. Let's go there and get some ice cream and coffee, and then I'll run you home.'

'I can walk.'

'I wouldn't mind seeing the Rutellis' villa. From the outside, I mean. Is it nice?'

'Very pleasant. And you can come in, if you want. The interior's really good. All of a piece.'

'Well, let's see how we feel.'

Zen obviously couldn't use any of his own credit cards, and his minders hadn't gone to the lengths of getting him any in his cover name. They had however provided an ample supply of large-denomination bank notes for his use, and he tossed a few of these on top of the bill before following Gemma outside.

It was now dark, the air mild and smooth as silk, the streets saturated with people standing or wandering about in animated clusters. Gemma and Zen joined them, she clacking along in her high-heeled beige sandals with delicate straps criss-crossing her feet and encircling her trim ankles. When they arrived at the *gelateria* they had a spirited argument about the appropriate choice of flavours. Zen attempted without success to enlist the owner's support in favour of his thesis that only fruit-based ice cream was healthy and proper at this time of year, and that by opting for hazelnut, pistachio and dark chocolate Gemma was making a fundamental dietary error which she would be lucky to live long enough to regret.

They took their overstuffed cones outside and sat licking them like a couple of children, giggling as they bent this way and that to try and avoid the melting ice cream from dripping on to their clothing. But behind Zen's mask of frivolity, he felt a little hollow. It was now clear what the situation was. Assuming that what Teresa Pananelli had said was even half true, then Gemma was a rapid recycler of summer lovers, and indeed possibly came to the beach at least partly with that in view. She seemed to like Zen, and he was certainly attracted to her. If he tried, they would probably end up going to bed together.

There was of course nothing whatever wrong with that, particularly for someone who hadn't been with a woman for over a year. Even the nuns who served as nurses at one of the sanatoria where he had stayed had started to look pretty good towards the end of his stay. The melancholy he could feel fermenting beneath his superficial gaiety was based on the clear and absolute realization that the affair would go no further than that. It would be a pleasant diversion, but no more. Afterwards they would go their separate ways, and the odds were that they would never meet again. And even if they did, nothing would come of it. Gemma had her own life, Zen his. And at their age, there was no force strong enough to fuse these disparate realities and bind them together for good.

When they had finished their ice creams, Gemma led the way back up the street to a blue sports-utility vehicle which she unlocked and then manoeuvred out of a space which from inside seemed slightly smaller than the automobile itself. They threaded their way at a respectful crawl through the crowd of pedestrians taking full advantage of their unwritten right of way, then turned off down a side street and worked their way back to the villa where Zen was staying. Gemma parked and turned off the motor.

'I think I will come in for a quick coffee after all, if that's all right.'

'That would be wonderful,' Zen replied.

Maybe I'm going to get lucky, he thought. His gloomy reservations of a few minutes earlier now seemed absurd. Why did he have to make everything so hard for himself? Other people just grabbed whatever they could, enjoyed themselves, and thought no more about it. What was he trying to prove by doing otherwise?

He walked up to the gate and was searching for his keys when a car door opened across the street and a man in uniform got out.

'*Buona sera,* signora, signore,' he said in a tone of voice which Zen recognized instinctively. Sure enough, as the man came closer and caught the light of the security lamp on the exterior of the villa, his uniform turned out to be that of a junior officer in the *carabinieri.* Zen returned the greeting guardedly.

'Signor Pier Giorgio Butani?' the man continued.

'Yes.'

'I'm sorry to disturb you at this hour, but my superior needs to ask you some questions regarding an investigation we have in progress. I must therefore ask you to accompany me to headquarters.'

Zen's first thought was that they had come for him, and this was an elaborate charade made necessary by Gemma's presence.

'Very well,' he said. 'In that case, I take it that you have no objection to Signora Santini going home.'

The *carabiniere* peered at Gemma for the first time.

'Gemma Santini?' he asked.

Gemma nodded.

'That's a stroke of luck. You're on the list too, signora. Do you want to take your car and follow me? That way you can go straight home afterwards.'

'What's all this about?' Gemma demanded tetchily.

'I expect they'll tell us that when we get there,' Zen told her soothingly.

He turned to the *carabinieri* officer.

'We'll follow you.'

'Very well. It's not far. Just keep my tail lights in view.'

Gemma walked back and unlocked her vehicle, then turned back to Zen, who was still standing where he had been before, staring into space.

'What's the matter?' she said, as the *carabiniere* revved up his motor.

Zen shook his head and walked over to her.

'I don't know. I just had this incredibly strong sense of déjà vu.'

'Get in,' Gemma said dismissively. 'Never mind your psychic experiences, let's just deal with whatever bullshit this is.'

'It can't be anything serious or they wouldn't have let us drive there.'

'Didn't you say you worked for the Ministry of the Interior? Why don't you show them your documents and tell them to stop messing us about?'

'These are the *carabinieri, cara*. Different force, different ministry, no love lost. If I tried to pull rank, they'd keep us there all night. See his signal light? He's turning left.'

'Yes, I do see it. I like you calling me *cara*, but I don't like you telling me how to drive.'

'I'll never do so again.'

'Yes, you will.'

They followed the lead car a few kilometres south along the *lungomare*, finally turning off into one of the uglier developments of what had obviously been coastal marshland until very recently. Signora Pananelli's husband would have been in his element here. Tower-block apartment buildings and hotels divided the space with huge parking lots and supermarkets. They stopped in front of a relatively modest, and by the standards of the place old, two-storey concrete block sporting the *carabinieri* crest above the doorway.

Their escort led the way upstairs and into a room where a man in the uniform of a major looked up briefly from the papers he was studying.

'Signor Giorgio Butani and Signora Gemma Santini,' the man who had accompanied them announced.

The officer at the desk nodded.

'Very good, Aldo. You may go.'

The door closed behind Aldo, but the *carabinieri* officer made no immediate move. Zen studied him with a professional eye. Competent but unambitious, with a huge pool of resentment at having been passed over in favour of more motivated rivals and stuck away here as the holiday cop in a town which, like Brigadoon, only came into existence for brief spells at long intervals, and vanished off the map the rest of the time. He would be pompous, long-winded and a stickler for the rule book. The way to deal with him was to take the initiative, but without getting too pushy.

'May we sit down?' Zen asked, bringing a chair for Gemma from those stacked against the wall.

'Of course, of course,' the officer replied without looking up. 'Please excuse me, I'll be with you in a moment. I just have to finish perusing this report.'

Like hell you do, thought Zen, fetching himself a chair and sitting beside Gemma. He gave her an encouraging smile. She was glaring in a manner which suggested that she might lose her patience very rapidly, which with a man like this would be fatal.

The *carabiniere* stacked the papers he had been reading neatly together and looked at them both.

'I'm sorry to have to bring you here so late . . .' he began.

'Your colleague already apologized,' interrupted Gemma tartly. 'What do you want with us?'

The major gave her a glance evidently intended as a warning.

'It concerns the death today of one Massimo Rutelli,' he said after a significant pause.

'We know about that,' Gemma returned. 'I heard that he had a stroke. What's that got to do with us?'

'There are various unresolved questions regarding the precise circumstances of the event which we are attempting to clarify. We have therefore compiled a list of all those clients of the bathing establishment where the body was discovered who were present on the beach today, with a view to interviewing them concerning what they may have seen or heard. Both your names appear on the said list.'

He pulled a notepad towards him.

'I propose to start with you, Signora Santini. You are resident in Lucca, I believe?'

'Yes.'

'At Via del Fosso number 73.'

'Correct.'

'You will be returning there tonight?'

It was said with just a hint of impertinent innuendo.

'Of course,' Gemma retorted.

'Then let us try and get you on your way as soon as possible, after which I will deal with your companion.'

'How do you know he's not coming with me?' demanded Gemma brazenly.

The *carabinieri* major gave her a look which Zen found himself quite unable to decipher. He seemed to be trying to think of a suitable answer to Gemma's question. Failing to do so, he ignored it and asked one himself.

'What time did you arrive at the beach today, signora?'

'I got there this morning at about ten and left again just before one, then returned after lunch.'

'According to the chart of the *bagno* drawn for us by the owner, Signor Rutelli apparently occupied the place immediately opposite yours.'

'Well, today he did. But in fact that's Pier Giorgio's place.'

She glanced at Zen, who leaned forward and cleared his throat.

'It is actually rented by the Rutelli family,' he said, 'but Girolamo, the elder brother, is an acquaintance of mine and gave me permission to use it. Massimo Rutelli evidently didn't know about this arrangement, so when he showed up unexpectedly he naturally took their usual spot.'

The major nodded absently, as this was merely a confirmation of old news.

'Did you see Signor Rutelli arrive?' he asked Gemma.

'No. I must have been sunning myself. But when I started sorting out my stuff before leaving, I noticed that there was someone else in Pier Giorgio's place.'

'Didn't you recognize him?'

'How could I? He was lying on his stomach with his face turned away from me. It could have been anyone.'

'So how did you know he wasn't Signor Butani?'

Gemma gave a throwaway gesture, as though this was obvious.

'His fingers.'

'What about his fingers?'

'They were thick and blunt. Women notice men's bodies a lot, they just don't notice them in the same way that men notice women's bodies. Pier Giorgio has very fine, tapering fingers. This man's were quite different. You could imagine them building a wall or castrating a horse. You couldn't imagine them caressing your skin.'

Zen looked away. For the first time he could remember, he was blushing. The major harrumphed.

'So the victim was present when you left shortly before one o'clock?'

'Yes.'

'And when you returned in the afternoon?'

'He was still there.'

'What time was that?'

Gemma shrugged.

'I went to the Bar Centrale and had a *panino* and some salad. About two, probably.'

She turned to Zen.

'What time did you get there?'

'I left home at one,' Zen replied. 'It takes about fifteen minutes to walk. I prefer the beach in the lunch hour. It's less crowded.'

'He was there when I arrived,' Gemma explained to the *carabiniere*. 'He'd taken the next place up and looked like he was asleep.'

'I was. I had lunch at home and finished off a bottle of Vermentino. As soon as I sat down on the beach, the heat just knocked me out.'

The major stood up, as if to impose his authority on this mutual dialogue.

'Please respect the sequence of questioning,' he said testily.

'I didn't realize there was one,' Gemma retorted.

Don't push him too far, thought Zen, but fortunately at that point the phone rang.

'Yes?' barked the *carabinieri* major. 'Very well. Tell them to wait.'

He hung up and turned to Gemma.

'We have established that, according to your testimony, Signora Santini, the victim arrived shortly before one o'clock and was still there at two. Is that correct?'

'Yes.'

'Did you notice a towel draped over his back?'

Gemma reflected for a moment.

'No, I don't think so. Wait a minute. There was one when I saw him in the afternoon. I'm not sure about the morning.'

'When did you leave the beach?'

'About four, earlier than usual. There was a rather unpleasant incident.'

Everything the major had picked up from his seemingly avid perusal of the chapter on basic interrogation techniques in the training manual now deserted him. He leaned forward, eyes bulging, all agog.

'What was that?'

Having achieved her effect, Gemma proceeded to dismiss it.

'Oh, nothing really. Pier Giorgio woke up at about three-thirty or so. I was going to get a coffee from Franco's bar, and I asked him if he'd like one too. On my way back, someone ran into me and spilt the coffee all over my bathing costume. I didn't have a spare with me, so there was nothing for it but to go home.'

'The man was running? Why?'

'I don't know. I mean, he wasn't running at first. He was just standing there on the boardwalk down the centre of Franco's strip. I thought he was staring at Pier Giorgio, to be honest.'

A gleam came into the major's eye.

'Are you sure it was Signor Butani he was staring at? Might it not have been Signor Rutelli, who was sitting in the next chair?'

Gemma made a moue of indifference.

'It could have been. I didn't have time to think about it. The next thing I knew, he'd whirled around and barged into me, spilling scalding coffee all over my belly and thighs.'

The major reflected a moment.

'Why did he run?'

'I haven't the slightest idea.'

'Was it because he heard you coming?'

'I don't think so. He was facing the other way, and I was barefoot so he couldn't have heard me. Besides, why should he be frightened of me?'

The major nodded and smiled the ironic, knowing smile of the master detective who alone has grasped the hidden clue concealed in the witness's seemingly ingenuous answer.

'Exactly. Why indeed should he be frightened of you?'

He turned to Zen.

'Did you notice this man, signore?'

'I saw him run off after he collided with Gemma, that's all.'

'Can either of you describe him?'

'No,' said Gemma decisively.

'You must remember something!' the major protested.

'Why? How many people do you think I see every day here? Hundreds, maybe a thousand, none of whom mean anything whatever to me. If I paid enough attention to them all to be able to describe them, I'd go mad. The man who ran into me was young, that's all I can tell you. And when you've said that, you've said everything. He looked young, he moved young, he acted young and he dressed young.'

'How young?'

Gemma shrugged and looked at Zen.

'Thirty?'

Zen nodded.

'Early thirties, I'd say.'

'That's right,' said Gemma. 'He was wearing jeans and a T-shirt with some writing on the front. In English.'

'He was English?' demanded the *carabinieri* officer.

'No, no. At least, I don't think so. He looked typically Italian, like any of the young Florentine *teppisti* who hang out down at Viareggio at the weekend.'

'Do you remember what this writing said?'

'Only one word.'

'What was that?'

' "Beach". *La spiaggia.* I recognized that from those signs the council put up everywhere in all the different European languages, warning people about the currents and all the rest of it. But there was another word I didn't get.'

' "Life",' said Zen unexpectedly.

The major regarded him with an air of professional triumph.

'Signor Butani, you have testified that you did not see this man until he was running away after his collision with Signora Santini. How then could you possibly have seen anything printed on the front of his clothing?'

'No, this wasn't him. Well, it might have been, I suppose, but it was later, after I left the beach. I was coming out of a shop in Via Puccini when I noticed some young man in a shirt like that. I didn't understand "beach", but the first word was "life's". That's the Anglo-Saxon genitive form, so the whole phrase must have been "A life's beach". *La vita della spiaggia.'*

His triumph at remembering this detail of English grammar from a long explanation once given to him by his American girlfriend Ellen was short-lived.

'*La spiaggia di una vita,*' Gemma corrected.

'It still doesn't make any sense!' the major rapped out.

'It's probably the name of some pop group,' said Gemma, rising. 'Well, is that all? Because if so I wouldn't mind getting home.'

'Just one more question. This is to both of you. Did either of you at any point during your time on the beach either hear or see anything unusual occurring in the immediate vicinity of your chairs?'

'Not apart from the incident I've mentioned,' said Gemma.

The major looked at Zen, who shook his head.

'No, that's all.'

'Very well. Signora Santini, you're free to go. Thank you for your cooperation and good night.'

He now sounded eager to be rid of her. Gemma bent towards Zen, who immediately stood up.

'Thanks for a wonderful evening,' she said.

'I'm glad you enjoyed it.'

'I really did, despite all this nonsense.'

'So did I.'

She pecked him briefly on both cheeks.

'See you tomorrow,' she said, and slipped out of the room.

Zen turned back to find the major regarding him with his knowing smile.

'I fear you may have to postpone that appointment, *dottore*,' he said.

Zen noted the title, which the *carabinieri* officer had not used before. He sensed that something was happening which he did not understand and could not control, for now at any rate.

'What more do you need from me?' he asked, sitting down again.

'Just a few brief questions.'

'But in that case I could have gone with Signora Santini!' Zen exclaimed, genuinely annoyed. 'She would have given me a lift. As it is, I'll have to call a taxi and . . .'

'No, you won't,' the major replied, sitting down heavily behind his desk.

He took a packet of cigarettes from a drawer and offered one to Zen, who accepted, mainly to see what this latest ploy forebode.

'Shortly after seven this evening,' the major went on, having lit their cigarettes, 'I received a phone call from my immediate superiors at provincial headquarters in Lucca. They relayed a message from their superiors at the Ministry in Rome, but I was given to understand that the original source lay still elsewhere.'

Zen smoked quietly and said nothing.

'The message was to the effect that a certain Pier Giorgio Butani, temporarily resident in this district, might fall within the scope of the murder enquiry I was undertaking.'

'What murder enquiry?'

'The one we've been discussing, *dottore*.'

'But Rutelli died of a stroke!'

'That's the story which the owner of the *bagno* in question has been putting out, for obvious reasons. We have made no official statement.'

'Rutelli was murdered?'

The major nodded.

'Shot once through the heart from very close range with a nine-millimetre pistol which was almost certainly silenced. The bullet was of the fragmenting type which breaks up inside the body, so there was no exit wound and very little bleeding. What there was was soaked up by the towel, which may have been placed there for that purpose. No one I have interviewed records having heard anything unusual, although many of them were sitting or lying just a few metres away. Nor does anyone recall a stranger going near the place where Rutelli was sitting, apart from the usual watermelon sellers and itinerant African merchants and the like. In short, it has all the hallmarks of a very professional job.'

Zen crushed out his cigarette.

'For reasons we won't go into, I have been staying for some time on the top floor of the Rutelli villa. The lower floor was unoccupied until yesterday, when I heard noises down there. This was presumably Massimo Rutelli arriving and settling in. For other reasons which need not concern us, I did not make myself known to him, and he clearly had no idea that I had been using the family's *ombrellone* at the beach. He therefore went there the next morning and settled in as usual. When I arrived, I saw someone in the place I had been using. I had no idea who it was, but since the place next to it had always been vacant during the week I sat down there instead. The towel was in place when I arrived, so Rutelli may already have been dead at that point. At no point did I hear or see anything remotely suspicious or untoward. Have you any other questions?'

The major sighed histrionically.

'There are numerous questions which I would very much like to put to you, *dottore*, but it has been made abundantly clear to me that this is not an option. Instead I have been instructed to turn you over to two operatives of a parallel authority who have driven up from Rome. That phone call earlier was to tell me that they have arrived.'

'Which parallel authority?'

The major gave him an unusually incisive look which made Zen realize the fatuity of his question.

'The persons concerned are waiting for you downstairs,' he remarked dismissively.

And there indeed they were, pacing the floor of the entrance hall to the *carabinieri* station, a man and a woman in their twenties, both unexceptionally dressed in civilian clothing. The only thing that announced their profession was the single quick glance they both gave Zen as he appeared on the stairs, head to toe and back up again, like executioners mentally measuring him for the drop.

The man turned away and started speaking into a portable radio. The woman walked up to Zen.

'We have a car outside,' she said, gesturing at the door.

Zen did not move.

'How do I know who you are?' he asked.

The woman smiled grimly.

'How do you think we know who you are, Dottor Zen?'

'Do you have identification?'

'If we did, it would be from the same source as the papers you have identifying you as Pier Giorgio Butani. And just as reliable.'

The man had finished his call.

'Come on!' he said. 'We've wasted enough time.'

A blue saloon was parked right outside the door. Another, in the middle of the street further down, flashed its headlights as they appeared. Once again Zen stopped dead, struck by the overwhelming sensation that all this had happened to him before. Tail lights, headlights . . . What was the connection?

He had no time to think about it, as his escorts bundled him into the waiting car, which immediately drove off through the sleeping town, ignoring traffic signs and lights. Five minutes later they were heading south on the A12 autostrada.

'Where are we going?' he asked the female agent, who had seated herself with him in the back of the car.

'Pisa,' she replied. 'From there you'll be flown to another destination.'

'Where?'

'We are not ordered to know.'

The car sped along the almost deserted freeway with its central divider of tall flowering bushes.

'But what about my things?' protested Zen. 'My clothes and personal possessions. They're all back at the villa in Versilia.'

'Someone will be sent to collect and pack them up and they will be forwarded to you in due course. In the meantime a supply of clothing and toiletries will be provided at your destination.'

Zen sighed in disgust.

'You might have given me some notice,' he said.

The woman turned to him.

'You don't seem to understand, *dottore*. The first we heard about all this was when Girolamo Rutelli contacted us with the news that his brother had been killed. He had been phoned by the authorities in Versilia, partly with a view to positively identifying the victim. Once we learned from him what had happened, we of course took urgent steps to remove you from the vicinity as soon as possible.'

'What have I got to do with it?'

'All the evidence suggests that the killing of Massimo Rutelli was a case of mistaken identity, and that you were the intended victim. The *modus operandi* was that of a classic professional hit. The implication is that the Mafia discovered where you were staying and made an attempt to silence you before you could testify against the Rizzo brothers in the States. Having failed, they would of course have tried again, possibly even tonight.'

The car swept through the automatic payment lane at the Pisa Centro exit and accelerated away along the dual carriageway leading to the airport. When the female agent spoke again, she sounded more conciliatory.

'Don't worry, *dottore*. The danger has passed. Wherever they're sending you next, you'll be well looked after.'

Islanda

It was when the light stopped dazzling him that Aurelio Zen realized that something odd had happened. He had ill-advisedly chosen a seat on the port side of the plane, so that the sun shone directly in on him, its low-inclined rays empowered with the brittle brilliance of February and the stultifying heat of August.

To make matters worse, it was all his own fault. The place he had originally been assigned was on the cool, shady, north-facing side of the plane, but this had not been apparent immediately after take-off, while the fat businessman in the next seat had been doing important things to a laptop computer. Spying an empty row of seats opposite, Zen had moved over, at which point the businessman promptly took possession of his original place and dumped all his voluminous gear in the place where he had been sitting. Theoretically, Zen supposed, he could call a cabin attendant and insist on being reseated in his rightful place, but it didn't seem worth the trouble. Along with everyone else, he had pulled down his blind when the cabin lights were turned off after lunch, but the insistent glow was still enough to bleach all substance from the ghostly figures cavorting about on the video screen in front of him.

Now, though, that intrusive radiance had disappeared. He raised the blind a fraction. No, the sun was no longer there. For a moment he wondered if it might have set, but the ocean vastness miles below still glittered in its reflected light. The sun must still be in the heavens, only it was now apparently aft of the plane. In which case they must be flying north. And even Zen's elementary knowledge of global geography included the information that America was not north of Europe.

He had spent the two weeks since his precipitate departure

from Versilia on the small island of Gorgona, thirty-five kilometres off the Tuscan coast, which was mainly occupied by a prison camp for non-violent juvenile offenders. Following his flight in a military helicopter from Pisa, Zen had been accommodated in a spare wing of the spacious quarters reserved for the director of the camp. The latter turned out to be a tall, perpetually stooping man with a whispery voice, diffident to the point of defensiveness, who – according to some camp lore which Zen later picked up from one of the warders – had been the principal of a college in Bari until certain rumours about the sexual activities of the staff and pupils came to the attention of the authorities. 'So he got a job with the *Grazia e Giustizia*, and they sent him here,' the man commented with a wry grin. 'It keeps him off the street corner back on the mainland, and he certainly can't corrupt these thugs. They'll corrupt him, if anything. One of them offered me a blow job the other day for a cigarette end I was about to throw in the toilet. "What would you do for a whole pack?" I asked him. The little bastard looked me in the eye and said, "No disrespect, *capo*, but I'm not sure you could handle that level of service all by yourself. Better invite a couple of your pals along."'

Zen ate his meals in the canteen, which served excellent food based on the products of the farm where the prisoners worked during the day. He had introduced himself to the staff as an academic ornithologist pursuing research into the behaviour of various rare local breeds of gulls. As he had hoped, the possibilities for conversational tedium opened up by this supposed professional interest ensured that no one ever addressed him. The rest of his time he spent exploring the maze of paths criss-crossing the island, which thanks to its 130-year vocation as a penal colony, remained completely unspoilt. The eastern slopes of the rugged interior were covered in pine forests like those which had once lined the coast, dimly visible through the haze to the east. Elsewhere, the prickly evergreen scrub of the *macchia* stretched as far as the eye could see, while occasional surviving groves of imported olives, holm oaks and sweet chestnuts provided shade. The air was utterly limpid, and as subtly perfumed as honey.

His idyll was disturbed only by thoughts of Gemma, and above all by the fact that he had been forced to leave so hurriedly, and was unable to contact her to explain why. All phone calls and correspondence had been strictly banned, so as far as Gemma was concerned Zen – or rather Pier Giorgio Butani – had simply vanished from Versilia overnight, without so much as a word of farewell. Even though he told himself repeatedly that the affair could never have amounted to anything, it remained a brutal, ugly and unsatisfying conclusion which left a very bitter taste behind.

He was entering his third week of seclusion when he received a message passed on by the director, instructing him to be packed and ready to leave at nine the following morning. Promptly at five minutes to that hour, a twin-rotor military helicopter identical to the one which had brought Zen to the island touched down in the parade ground where the inmates of the prison camp had to assemble each morning for their roll call and work assignments. He trudged across the concrete towards it, lugging the bags which had been shipped over on the ferry from Livorno shortly after his arrival. The sun was bright and clear in the cloudless sky, the air sweet and fresh, and until the helicopter's arrival the silence had been absolute. Zen felt as if he were being exiled from a paradise to which he could never return.

A matter of minutes later they were back at Pisa, at the military end of the airport, away from the commercial terminal. Here Zen was led to a small fixed-wing jet aircraft with no markings. His baggage was placed in the hold while he climbed a set of fold-down steps to the interior. This consisted of a single cabin with comfortable chairs facing a low central table. Seated in one of these was the young diplomat who had visited Zen during his convalescence.

He immediately stood up, shook hands with Zen and showed him into a seat, then produced a flask of excellent coffee and two cups. A moment later the stepladder was folded up, the door closed and the engines started.

'Forgive the rudimentary cabin service,' Zen's companion said as the aircraft started to taxi. 'On the other hand, the accommodation is superior to what you're likely to have for the rest of your journey, and at least you won't have to listen to the usual sermon about what to do in the unlikely event of a landing on water. I wonder if anyone's life has ever been saved by one of those cheap life-jackets they stuff away under the seats. It seems to me that all those safety announcements do is spread an irrational fear of flying, actually one of the safest forms of transport. Imagine if every time you got into a bus or train or taxi you had to listen to a lot of euphemistic waffle about what to do if the thing crashed! No one would ever leave home.'

The aircraft veered jerkily to the right, the engines roared, and before Zen knew it they were off the ground. He watched the coastline turning into a map for several minutes, then turned back to his companion, who was filling their cups of coffee. When he looked up at Zen, his professional mask was firmly back in place.

'I trust your stay on Gorgona was tolerable?' he said.

'Very pleasant, thank you.'

'It seemed the best short-term solution, given the events in Versilia.'

He looked at Zen with a serious expression.

'You're a very lucky man. The Mafia have now tried twice to kill you, and failed both times. Very few people can say that.'

'Is it certain that I was the intended target?'

The young diplomat gestured dismissively.

'*Dottore*, there has never been a recorded case of a murder on the beach in that area. A few knifings late at night down at the Viareggio end, and the odd settling of accounts between drug gangs, but otherwise nothing. Then a corporate lawyer with no known enemies, seated in the place which you had occupied for several weeks, is shot through the heart at point-blank range with a silenced pistol in broad daylight by a killer who nevertheless completely evades attention, even though the *bagno* was packed at the time.'

Zen nodded.

'I suppose you're right.'

'Of course we are. Which is why we've decided to move you yet again, this time to the United States.'

Catching Zen's look of alarm, he held up a soothing hand.

'The trial's not due to start for some time, but the safest option in the meantime seemed to be to get you out of the country and into the hands of the federal authorities. They have a lot of experience in protecting witnesses, and America is a very large country. To make matters even more secure, we are flying you not to New York, where the trial will take place, but to the west coast. There you'll be met by Italian-speaking agents of the FBI who will meet you airside, bypass all the immigration and customs procedures, and escort you to a safe house in a location which hasn't been disclosed even to us. It will be impossible for the Mafia to find you there.'

Zen looked out of the window again. The aircraft was passing over the Apennine chain. They were sending him away. He suddenly felt very small and helpless and desolate.

'Our immediate destination is Malpensa,' the diplomat continued. 'There you will transfer to the regular Alitalia flight to Los Angeles. You will be boarded separately from the other passengers, and without passing through passport control and all the other nonsense, and seated in the business-class cabin. I take it that you packed your bags yourself, that they have not been out of your possession at any time since then, and that they do not contain any explosive or inflammable substances.'

It was only after Zen had solemnly shaken his head that he realized that this had been intended as a joke.

'Have you any questions?' his companion enquired urbanely.

Zen thought for a moment.

'Yes,' he said. 'If I write a letter, will you post it for me?'

The diplomat looked embarrassed.

'That would depend,' he replied.

'On what?'

'On whom you wished to write to and on what you intended to say.'

'In other words, you would have to read it.'

The young man gestured in a pained way.

'Somebody would,' he said. 'There's no point in trying to conceal that. There's a lot at stake in this operation in terms of national honour and prestige. I'm afraid it would be naive to pretend that any obvious precautions are going to be overlooked out of motives of delicacy.'

Zen nodded.

'Thank you for being candid. You could have lied. It doesn't matter, anyway. It was a stupid idea.'

When they arrived at Malpensa, Zen was transferred to an airport authority car and taken to a windowless lounge in a remote wing of the terminal. Here he had been left to cool his heels for over an hour, before being led back to the car and driven along a succession of vast concrete taxiways to a parked Alitalia 747 which was loading the in-flight food and beverage trolleys. Zen was loaded too, via a stepped ramp which was wheeled up to the aircraft's rear door. It all reminded him oddly of his experience on his return from Malta to Sicily, where he had been 'met at the airport' – a strip of abandoned motorway – by members of the Ragusa Mafia for delivery to Don Gaspare Limina. Once again, he was just a package, to be shunted around and stowed away, just like the packages of drugs unloaded from the Malta flight. Packages don't have feelings or opinions about the process this involves or their ultimate destination. Zen did, but they were equally irrelevant.

Some three hours later, twisting uncomfortably in his seat and worrying about the disappearance of the sun, these views had not changed. The prospect of finding himself in America filled him with terror. Like many Italians of his generation, he had never been abroad before, apart from day trips into Austria, Switzerland and recently Malta. He had never even owned a passport, and it seemed highly appropriate that the one he was now carrying should be in a false name. *Il bel paese* could offer the traveller every conceivable variety of landscape, climate, natural beauties and cultural treasures. Why waste a lot of time going to some foreign country where they used funny money, spoke some barbaric dialect, and couldn't be relied upon to make a decent cup of coffee, still less know how to cook pasta properly? It was a stupid idea, however you looked at it. And if the foreign country in question was on the other side of the Atlantic Ocean, it became quite literally insane.

Zen's rule of thumb in these matters was very simple. In theory, at least, he was prepared to consider going to any country which had formed part of the Roman Empire. If it had also been part of the political or trading empire of the Venetian Republic, so much the better. Egypt, Turkey, Bulgaria, Greece, the Balkans, Austria, Bavaria, France, Iberia, North Africa – even England, at a pinch – he could contemplate as a hypothetical destination. Beyond those limits, he just didn't see the point. The Romans had been brutal bastards, but they were no fools. If they hadn't bothered to conquer Sweden or Poland, there was probably a good reason. And they certainly hadn't been to America. Maybe they didn't know it was there. Or perhaps they'd heard rumours, but just didn't care enough to investigate further. Either way, Zen was inclined to trust their judgement.

As if this wasn't enough to stoke his anxiety, there was the small matter of his testimony at the trial. The Ragusa thugs who had delivered Zen to Don Gaspare Limina had been given to understand that he would be killed, and so they had not bothered to conceal their faces. But thanks to the Catania clan's mercy, or rivalry, he had survived to find himself in the almost unprecedented position for a non-mafioso of being able to identify two prominent members of 'those pushy little squirts from Ragusa', as Limina had contemptuously referred to his upstart neighbours.

But life is a moving target, and never more so than for Mafia *capi*. Don Gaspare had been arrested in the course of a massive operation following the attempt on Zen's life, and was now serving a multiple life sentence in a particularly cold and primitive prison high in the mountains near Matera. Meanwhile Bernardo 'The Tractor' Provenzano, the last remaining Corleonesi chieftain, still unapprehended after almost forty years as a fugitive, had managed to impose his control on the relatively free market and regional competition which had started to evolve following the breakdown of the old hierarchies. Following a spate of violent deaths and a judicious selection of the classic unrefusable offers, the Ragusa clan had been brought under his control, but also under his protection. Whoever testified against Nello and Giulio Rizzo would be testifying against Cosa Nostra itself, and would be a marked man for the rest of his days.

For a while Zen toyed with the idea that maybe they weren't going to America after all, given that they seemed to be flying north, but a glance at the route map in the Alitalia magazine dispelled this illusion. It appeared that when aeroplanes went from place to place, they never did so directly, but took a long curving roundabout path by way of such outlandish localities as Baffin Island and Labrador. Perhaps it had something to do with the prevailing winds, as in the days of sailing ships. Or maybe it was a planned diversion designed to give everyone a chance to get some sleep. Overnight trains often went deliberately slowly so as not to arrive at some ungodly hour and decant the passengers half awake at a deserted station in a slumbering city.

He flipped through the magazine, pausing to skim an article about the city he was bound for. Apparently it had originally been settled by the Spanish, who named it *El Pueblo de Nuestra Señora la Reina de Los Angeles*. There was a translation in Italian, 'The Town of Our Lady the Queen of the Angels', and photographs of an old stone monastery gleaming white in the sunlight. Maybe Los Angeles wouldn't be so bad after all, he thought. It sounded like a pleasant, old-fashioned sort of place, and at least the people would all be Catholics. Although by no means a committed believer, Zen preferred to be surrounded by his own sort. Protestants were an enigma to him, all high ideals one minute and ruthless expediency the next. You knew where you were in a Catholic culture: up to your neck in lies, evasions, impenetrable mysteries, double-dealing, back-stabbing and underhand intrigues of every kind. With which comforting thought he lowered the blind again and dozed off.

The next thing he knew was being woken by the stewardess and asked to fasten his seatbelt for landing. Were they there already? Ten hours, the captain had said before take-off. Surely he hadn't been asleep that long? The cabin lights had been turned on and the other passengers looked restive, all except the businessman who had taken Zen's seat after he moved. He was sprawled back, his chair in full recline position, a blackout mask over his eyes and his mouth wide open as if snoring. The cabin attendant in the other aisle bent over him and said something and then, not getting any response, buckled up the man's safety belt.

The scene outside the window looked like nothing on earth, a rough first draft of creation fresh from the drawing board: deep ocean rollers going about their restless immemorial business, then breaking up in spectacular confusion on the ragged coastline, and beyond that an uneven wasteland torn to shreds by outcrops and crags of raw rock breaking the surface in random profusion. There were no buildings, no fields, no farms, no roads, no people. Nothing.

This was not how Zen had imagined America, but as the wheels touched down and they rolled to a roaring halt, he saw a row of large camouflaged military jets, each with the United States flag painted on the tail. They continued to taxi for some time, then drew to a halt. The sound of the engines died away and everyone stood up.

Zen manoeuvred his way politely through the throng towards the row of seats opposite, where his hand baggage was in the overhead locker. The man who had taken his seat was still lying there, mouth agape. He had had several rounds of cocktails and liqueurs before and after the lunch which Zen himself had refused after one glance, and was no doubt still sleeping them off.

Gradually the line of standing passengers started moving slowly forward, carrying Zen with it. The crew members at the door nodded, smiled, apologized, and assured everyone that the delay would be a brief one. It seemed to Zen that one of the male attendants, a slim young man with piercing eyes, gave him a particularly meaningful look, but that was neither here nor there. Everyone knew that *i steward* were all gay. Outside, the light seemed diminished, uncertain of itself. The air was harder than he was used to, almost fibrous in texture, and smelt strongly of seaweed. Zen wrapped his coat about him and stepped down the gangway to the waiting bus.

A short drive brought them to a low line of concrete buildings, where they were unloaded into what looked to Zen like the dance hall of a 'youth club' to which the church was trying to attract the disaffected teenagers of some no-hope town in Calabria. The unsmiling uniformed blonde men and women who had accompanied them on the bus now escorted them inside, then closed and locked the doors and drove away in the bus.

One of the side effects of Zen's brush with death had turned out to be that his lifelong fear of flying had been dispelled. This may have been due to the greater fears to which he had been exposed, or simply a case of familiarity breeding contempt; aeroplanes had been the preferred means of transport of the authorities in whose hands he had been ever since the 'incident'. At all events, he had now come to realize that flying was not at all frightening, just massively boring. And the most boring parts were not the flight itself, but the bits before it started and after it stopped. Entering the United States was evidently not going to be an exception. There was no sign of any passport officers, no sign of the luggage, no purposeful activity at all. Everyone just stood around.

Five minutes later, a second busload of passengers returned from the plane to swell the waiting throng, and some time after that a third, bearing a final contingent of stragglers. Meanwhile a tanker truck had approached the aircraft, and men in orange jumpsuits were hooking up a coil of large plastic piping to its underbelly. Zen turned to a young man standing next to him who had just finished a long mobile-phone call in Italian.

'Looks like they're filling her up,' he remarked, as a token conversational opening.

The man looked him blankly.

'Emptying her out, you mean. Christ knows when we'll get to LA at this rate. My people are going ballistic.'

He punched more buttons and turned away.

'At first I thought it was a joke!' said a voice to Zen's left. 'Only on Alitalia!'

The speaker was a woman of fifty-something whose crisply tailored coat merely emphasized the puffiness of her features.

'Imagine diverting an international flight for a thing like that in this day and age!' she went on, rubbing her pudgy fingers together. 'It's just a joke, a bad joke!'

Having failed to get a reply, the man Zen had spoken to first snapped his phone shut.

'The flight had over seven hours to go, there are three hundred and seventy-something passengers and crew aboard, and all but one of the lavatories were out of action. Think about it, signora. The alternative would have been no joke at all.'

The woman wrinkled her nose in disgust.

'I prefer not to think about such things,' she declared haughtily. 'It's disgusting, just disgusting. Only on Alitalia!'

An ambulance had now pulled up to the steps leading to the front of the aircraft. Two paramedics got out, unloaded a stretcher from the rear doors, and carried it up into the plane. Zen was desperate for a cigarette, and the woman's mention of lavatories, whatever it might have been intended to mean, made him realize that he might be able to get away with smoking one there. Looking around, he spotted two doors marked with the universal symbols for men and women.

Ten minutes later, with two *Nazionali*-worth of nicotine coursing through his blood, he emerged a changed man, totally confident about whatever questions the US immigration officials were going to throw at him, despite the fact that his FBI escort apparently hadn't shown up to whisk him through these formalities as had been promised. The only problem was that the immigration people apparently hadn't shown up either. In fact there was no sign of any activity whatsoever. All the passengers were just standing around looking glum, and staring at the men working on the plane from the tanker. Zen tried asking one of the uniformed blondes what was going on, but he or she would only reply in English, which Zen couldn't understand.

They had been there over an hour, during which time Zen made three further trips to the lavatory, when he heard someone calling what sounded like 'Pier Giorgio Butani!'. The speaker was another of the uniformed clones, and Zen's first thought was that that he was going to get arrested for smoking in a non-designated area. Then he realized that what must have happened was that the FBI agents had finally arrived. He showed his passport to the man, who nodded and gestured to Zen to follow him.

He was led through the crowd of passengers, all of whom looked at him with a mixture of curiosity and envy for having been singled out for special exemption from this communal purgatory. Zen gave them a politely superior smile. They went through a door and along a corridor, then into an office where two people were seated. One was a very striking young woman with the natural pale blonde hair which seemed to be as common here as it was rare in Italy. Zen's escort handed her the passport and then left. The other person was a thin, balding man in his late thirties with the startled expression of one who has been unexpectedly woken from deep sleep. He was wearing a hideous brown acrylic suit, battered ankle-length boots, a pink button-down shirt and a patterned yellow tie. The woman wore a dark blue uniform and white blouse buttoned at the collar. She rose and handed Zen a card which read: 'Þórunn Sigurðardòttir', with a line of incomprehensible script and some phone numbers beneath.

The man also stood up, searching in his pockets.

'I should also have a card somewhere,' he said in heavily accented Italian. 'Maybe in my wallet. No, I must have left them in my other jacket. Wait a minute!'

He finally produced a crumpled business card with a telephone number and someone's name written on it.

'Sorry, other side,' the man told Zen, who turned the card over. It was embossed in blue and gold with the words 'Gruppo Campari: Campari, Cinzano, Cynar, Asti Cinzano, Riccadonna. Snæbjörn Guðmundsson.'

'What's Campari got to do with it?' asked Zen.

'That's just my private business card,' the man explained. 'I'm also the Italian consul here.'

He indicated the uniformed woman.

'Signora Sigurðardòttir is a police officer. She wishes to ask you a few questions. I will translate. Please sit here.'

Zen took a chair facing the desk and the interview began. The form was invariable: the woman spoke in a language utterly alien to Zen, the man followed with a question in Italian, Zen answered, the man spoke to the woman in the language she had used, and she made notes on a pad open in front of her.

'Signor Butani, I have already spoken to members of the crew on this flight. I have been given to understand by them that you were boarded ahead of all the other passengers, and through a separate entrance, bypassing the normal controls.'

'Yes.'

'Why was this?'

'I have recently spent several months in hospital, recuperating after a serious accident. The ground staff had been informed of this fact, and kindly arranged for me to be given priority boarding.'

'What kind of accident?'

'A car crash.'

'What injuries did you sustain?'

'Serious concussion, head injuries, compression injuries to chest including two fractured ribs and a collapsed lung, limb fractures requiring pinning, plus the usual assortment of relatively minor fractures, lacerations and contusions.'

'Yet you now appear to be fully mobile.'

'The accident occurred almost a year ago. I still suffer from limb stiffness and some psychological effects, particularly when forced to spend long hours in a small, crowded space such as an aircraft. Fortunately I had contacts at Alitalia who were able to ensure that I was not inconvenienced any more than was strictly necessary.'

The female officer made lengthy notes. She was stunningly beautiful, Zen thought abstractly, and would certainly have cut a wide swathe through the herds of *ragazzi* on any Italian street. But somehow her beauty remained purely theoretical. He didn't feel remotely interested or excited by her.

'Do you have your boarding pass, please?' þórunn Sigurðardòttir asked.

Zen found it in his wallet and handed it over.

'This identifies your seat number as 24A,' the woman said.

'Yes.'

'But I understand from the crew members I interviewed that you were in fact seated in 25F.'

That's right. There was someone sitting in the next seat to

61

mine, and he didn't really seem the sort of person I wanted to be beside for ten hours unless I had to. The plane wasn't full, and I spotted an empty seat on the other side of the cabin, so once we were airborne I moved over there.'

'And the passenger who had been sitting next to you then took your original seat, is that correct?'

'It is. May I ask why any of this is of the slightest significance?'

The uniformed woman spoke rapidly in her incomprehensible tongue. It didn't sound to Zen's ears much like English – it was probably some regional American dialect, he supposed – but he had no difficulty in understanding the tone of voice. This was confirmed when the consul translated.

'Signora Sigurðardòttir has indicated that she wishes you to confine yourself to answering her questions.'

Zen beamed ingratiatingly.

'Please assure *la signora ispettrice* of my willingness to cooperate to the full with her enquiry, whatever it may concern.'

Snæbjörn Guðmundsson duly translated, or at least said something to the woman, who had been eyeing Zen sharply. She nodded, then asked another question.

'What is the purpose of your journey to the United States?'

'Business.'

'What kind of business?'

Here Zen paused for the first time, at a loss how to answer. On the one hand, this woman was an accredited member of an American law-enforcement body, and therefore entitled to the truth. On the other, she had accepted Zen's passport in his cover name at its face value, and therefore evidently wasn't of a sufficiently high status to have been briefed about the real purpose of his trip. As usual, the safest option seemed to be a lie.

He justified the pause with a laugh.

'I was just wondering how best to describe it, but actually it's very similar to that of the consul here, except that I deal in much less well-known names. High-quality olive oils, cheeses, dried mushrooms, honeys and preserves from small organic producers. It's a low-volume, high-mark-up business. If the restaurants and boutique stores want the best, they have to come to me, but equally I have to come over every so often to . . .'

Þórunn Sigurðardòttir held up her hand and Zen turned off the flow.

'Do you have any commercial competitors?'

'Virtually none. As I said, this is very much a niche market, and I've just about cornered it.'

'What about personal enemies?'

'None that I know of.'

The woman made more notes whose length seemed out of all proportion to Zen's replies. Then she raised her startling blue eyes to Snæbjörn Guðmundsson and spoke at some length.

The consul stood up and looked at Zen.

'Let's go,' he said.

'What about my passport?'

'She needs to keep it for now. I'll explain outside.'

Zen assumed that this meant outside in the corridor, or at best back in the packed lounge with the other waiting passengers, but to his surprise Guðmundsson led the way through a set of double doors into the fresh air.

And fresh it was, too! Tangy, salted gusts swept across the car park in front of them with such boisterous energy that they almost knocked the two men over. The consul pointed to the left and strode off towards a small red Fiat which he unlocked. Zen stowed his cabin bag in the boot and got in to the car.

'Now then, I think it's time I explained the situation,' Snæbjörn Guðmundsson said when they were sheltered from the wind.

'It's time someone did,' Zen replied pointedly.

'Feel free to smoke,' Guðmundsson remarked. 'I can smell it on your clothing. A very pleasant odour which brings back happy memories of my misspent youth. No thanks, I've given up myself, but I remain a child of the Sixties. È proibito proibire and all that. So please go ahead.'

Zen lit a cigarette and rolled down the window slightly, creating an instant gale inside the car. The consul closed Zen's window and opened his own, on the leeward side.

'As you know,' he said, 'your flight was diverted here due

to technical causes of a routine nature. Normally it would just have been a question of a few hours' delay at most for the necessary maintenance work to take place. But at the point when the passengers were being disembarked to facilitate this work – unblocking toilets can be a very smelly business – one of them failed to respond to the directions of the cabin crew. A doctor was summoned and subsequently pronounced him dead.'

'The one who was sitting in my place,' said Zen.

'Exactly. A certain Angelo Porri. This has placed the authorities here in a very difficult position. They of course have no wish to delay anyone's journey any longer than is necessary, but in the unlikely event that the cause of death turns out not to have been natural, everyone who was on board the plane will naturally become an important witness if not a potential suspect.'

'Yes, I see.'

'The corpse has been taken to a hospital in the city, where it will shortly undergo a post-mortem. Once that is concluded, you and your fellow passengers will most likely be free to leave.'

'And in the meantime?'

'For the time being, the rest of the passengers will remain in the holding area. They will be told that the repairs are taking longer than had been anticipated.'

Zen braved the wind long enough to throw his butt out of the window.

'So I'm being singled out for special treatment. Why?'

Snæbjörn Guðmundsson started the engine.

'This afternoon I received two telephone calls relating to my position as Italian consul. This in itself was highly unusual. I have to say that the position is an honorary one which I fill partly because it gives me a certain cachet in business and government circles here that is useful to my job with the Gruppo Campari. Even that is largely a part-time activity. My real work is quite different.'

'And what's that?'

'I'm an artist.'

They drove out of the car park on to a dual-carriageway road.

'The first call was from the police here at the airport,' Snæbjörn Guðmundsson went on. 'They explained that an Alitalia flight had been diverted . . .'

'That's the second time you've used that word,' Zen pointed out. 'Diverted from where?'

'From its flight in mid-Atlantic, of course.'

Zen laughed.

'So what is this, Atlantis?'

'This is Iceland.'

'I don't see any ice.'

'No, Greenland's the icy one. Some people say the original settlers deliberately named them like that, so as to send potential invaders to the wrong address. At any rate, as I was saying, the first call I received was from the airport authorities. They simply asked me to be prepared to come out to Keflavik in case any of the Italian passengers required assistance or refused to reboard the plane. People sometimes react in odd ways to emergency landings, even if the reason is completely routine.'

'Someone said the lavatories were blocked. How did that happen?'

'The mind boggles. But apparently they were, and you can imagine what the result would have been. Anyway, the really interesting call I got was the second one. That was from the Foreign Ministry in Rome, which just about knocked me over. From time to time someone from the embassy in Copenhagen pops up to check that I'm not fiddling my expenses, but as far as direct contact goes that's about it. And here was a senior official at the Ministry – I didn't catch his name, but you could tell by his manner that he wasn't a subordinate – phoning me in person to brief me about a certain Dottor Pier Giorgio Butani who was travelling to Los Angeles on the diverted plane.'

Zen looked stolidly out of the window at the landscape through which they were passing, an undifferentiated jumble of jagged rocks of every size and shape separated by patches of boggy moor.

'What did they tell you about me?' he asked at last.

'Just that you were a VIP and that I was to accord you every possible assistance and protection during your enforced stopover here. I am not quite sure what they meant by "protection", but since it now appears that the delay to your flight may not be as brief as was first thought, I have obtained permission from the police to spare you a return to that squalid waiting area and take you somewhere more comfortable. þórunn Sigurðardòttir will call on my cellphone if the flight's cleared for departure, and I can have you back at the airport in twenty minutes.'

They were now entering the outskirts of a settlement whose planned sprawl was more orderly but no more attractive than that of the eroded lava fields through which they had just passed. It all looked quiet, neat, functional and dull. These outer suburbs were succeeded by an older section, equally sterile and monotonous, but with buildings of stone and brick rather than concrete.

They went to a café on a pedestrianized street in what appeared to be the centre. Some people at the next table were eating slabs of pallid fish or meat smothered in an anonymous sauce, with boiled potatoes and a scattering of shrivelled vegetables. Zen thought longingly of the lasagne and the beef he had turned up his nose at on the plane, then ordered a cheese sandwich and a beer and tried to collect his thoughts. Despite his earlier volubility, Snæbjörn Guðmundsson now seemed quite prepared just to sip his coffee and not interrupt this process. Indeed, most of the other couples in the café were sitting in a profound but seemingly unstressful silence which in Italy would have been the height of bad form.

There was a lot of information to process. First of all, he was in a remote northern country of which he knew absolutely nothing, starting with its exact geographical location. Secondly, the man who had taken his seat on the plane was now dead of causes as yet unknown. The parallels with the fate of Massimo Rutelli were disturbingly obvious, although fortunately not as yet to the Icelandic police. Thirdly, it was unclear when or even whether he would be free to resume his journey, and what action if any his sponsors at the Foreign Ministry might take about this. But what was finally most disturbing was that there was absolutely nothing that he could personally do to affect the outcome. Such powerlessness induced both frustration and anxiety. Zen had always found that happiness came from throwing himself into some activity, even if it turned out later to have been futile. Work was relaxing, whereas this enforced, problematic and conditional idleness threatened to wreck his nerves in no time at all.

He had just reached this dispiriting conclusion when a series of loud electronic beeps sounded out the opening strains of the Italian national anthem. The other patrons of the café turned with expressions of icy disapproval towards Snæbjörn Guðmundsson, who plucked out his cellphone and bolted for the door. An elderly man at the next table with a head like a block of wood squared off with an axe, prolific silver-black hair, the regulation-issue laser-blue eyes, monster teeth and no neck at all looked at Zen and said something incomprehensible but evidently uncomplimentary. Zen instinctively spread his palms wide, tossed his head back, shrugged, and replied 'Eh, eh, eh, eh, eh, eh, eh, eh!', thus indicating that while he entirely agreed with the other man's deprecation of the indiscriminate use of mobile phones in public places, he was not his brother's keeper, still less Snæbjörn Guðmundsson's, and couldn't be held responsible for the latter's thoughtlessness. The Icelander regarded this pantomime with growing alarm, then pointedly turned his back.

Zen followed suit, looking out of the plate-glass window to the street, where Guðmundsson was talking animatedly into the phone under the scrutiny of some swarthy vagrant standing barely a metre away and staring intently up at him. Finally the consul concluded his conversation and returned inside.

'Bad news, I'm afraid,' he said, sitting down at their table again. 'The results of the post-mortem were inconclusive. They want to consult the senior pathologist at the university, but he's away at a conference and won't return until tomorrow.'

'You mean we all have to stay here until then?'

'Not all. The police have decided that if a crime has taken place, the passengers seated outside the cabin in which the victim was seated can be ruled out. They and the crew are being allowed to leave tonight. The others, including you, must remain until a final verdict has been reached on the cause of death.'

Zen sighed disgustedly.

'But you have your orders from the Farnesina!' he protested. 'To expedite my departure in any way you can.'

'Unfortunately that exceeds my powers. All I can do is to offer you a comfortable bed and hospitality at my house until this matter is sorted out. I suggest we go there now, unless you'd like to return with me to the airport to collect your bags. They have been unloaded from the hold and are in storage.'

Zen thought for a moment.

'Did you tell the police that I would be staying with you?' he demanded.

'Yes. They naturally wanted to be assured of your where-abouts.'

'Who was that street person who was listening in to your conversation?'

'Who do you mean?'

'Some low-life standing there right beside you, listening to every word you said. You must have seen him.'

'I didn't. I was probably paying too much attention to what the police were telling me. But what about him?'

Zen shrugged.

'Nothing, probably. He just disturbed me somehow. I don't want everyone in town knowing where I'm going to be sleeping this evening.'

Snæbjörn Guðmundsson stared at him.

'You have reason to believe that you're in danger?' he asked.

Zen realized that he'd stumbled.

'A man in my position inevitably makes a lot of enemies,' he replied blandly. 'But never mind, I'm probably imagining the whole thing. I'm afraid this unexpected visit here has rather shaken me.'

'Of course, of course! So then, will you come with me, or go straight to my house?'

'Neither. I'd like to go out and walk around a bit, then meet you at your house later. I need some exercise, and some time to think.'

Guðmundsson looked doubtful for a moment, then nodded resignedly.

'Very well.'

He got out his wallet.

'I'd better give you some money.'

'I can change some.'

'Not at this time of night.'

Zen glanced at the window again.

'What time is it?' he asked.

'A quarter to nine.'

'But when does it get dark?'

'It doesn't. The sun just dips briefly below the horizon around midnight and then comes up again about two in the morning. In between, there's a couple of hours of dusk, but no darkness. In the winter, of course, it's the other way round.'

He wrote something on the back of the receipt returned by the waitress, and handed it to Zen along with a couple of banknotes.

'That's my address and phone number,' he said. 'Just hand it to a taxi driver when you've had enough, or call me if you want company.'

Outside in the street, they separated. Zen drifted off, wondering at the invariable grey light. Summer days here in the north evidently didn't have the classic three-act structure that he'd grown up with. They just maundered on like some experimental film in which the whole point is that nothing ever happens. It was then that Aurelio Zen decided to do something he had not done for a very long time indeed, so long that the person who had done it seemed almost as much of a stranger as the genetically modified strangers thronging by in the street. He decided to get quite deliberately and totally drunk.

He took out the banknotes which the consul had given him. They came to fifty thousand *kronur*, whatever that might amount to. He went into the first bar he came to and ordered a vodka. This was not something he normally drank, but it was one of those useful international products, like taxis, which were available everywhere and always called the same thing in every language. The vodka was served ice cold in a small shot glass. Zen downed three of them in short order, then headed out to the streets in search of more bars.

He found them quite easily. Indeed, after a while they began to find him. They were all more or less the same; dingy, poky, smelly little burrows with bad lighting and deafening music. But after a while he started to feel quite at home, despite the fact that the other clients were all half a metre taller than him and at least twenty years younger, with the studiously bored air of modern youth everywhere. On the streets he had noticed more of the short, dark, unkempt people like the one he had seen eavesdropping on Snæbjörn Guðmundsson's phone conversation, but they didn't seem to come into the bars. Couldn't afford the prices, probably. They looked a bit like the East European refugees and migrants flooding into Italy from Albania and Romania, another race entirely, wearing clothes from another era.

That was outside, though, where Zen no longer had any desire to go. He'd found a cosy nook at the back of a subterranean den where a few youngsters were half-heartedly dancing, and a lissom blonde refilled his shot glass as soon as he emptied it.

Later on the action on the dance floor hotted up considerably, until Zen seemed to be the only person in the place not flinging himself about to the battering rhythms of the sound system. Several of the girls were now dancing topless, their breasts jiggling about in a touching, natural, slightly comical way. Their partners too had stripped down to the absolute minimum. The air was heavy with the smell of sweat and testosterone.

Later still, the place was half empty, the lissom blonde ignored him, and the lights came brutally to life. Zen consulted his watch, but it was still on Italian time. Anyway, they were evidently closing. He got to his feet and shuffled over to the door. The streets were even more packed than the bar had been earlier. No one was dancing, but a couple of drunken scuffles broke out and were quickly subdued. The little, dark, shabbily dressed people were much in evidence too, looking on at the proceedings with that sly, half-mocking expression they all had.

Zen's first priority was to find a taxi and get himself driven to the consul's house, but that was not so simple. The streets where he was were all pedestrianized, and his enquiries were either ignored or elicited a broad gesture and a string of verbiage he couldn't understand. In the end he set off walking along the main street, confident that sooner or later he would find a taxi rank.

Then, out of the corner of his eye, he saw a car in a side street with an illuminated sign on top. Someone was getting out of it. Zen started to run, but he was still some way away when the taxi revved up and drove quickly away. The person who had got out of it entered a nearby block of flats and closed the door. Disheartened, Zen turned back towards the main street. He was still some twenty metres away from it when the figure came rushing at him out of an alley to his right, a knife in its hand.

Zen's drunkenness saved him initially. He was so startled that he fell over backwards, landing heavily on his buttocks as the assailant swerved past. It was one of the little dark men he had been seeing all evening. He turned now, the knife held out, and walked back to where Zen was lying sprawled on the paving stones. The blade of the knife gleamed in the light from the nearest street lamp, but the man's face was in shadow.

Tackling a man on the ground is a tricky business. You have to stoop to his level to get anything done, and if you do you lose your only advantage. Aurelio Zen was aware of this, having been in this situation before, but playing the other role. His attacker, oddly enough, was also aware of it. He made no further berserk moves, did not hurl himself on his prone victim, just stood there, sizing up the situation.

Zen was still drunk, but drunks can often focus very effectively on just one thing, which was all he had to do at present. So when the dark figure made its move, aiming a kick at Zen's ribs, he was ready. He flipped over, away from the blow, and was on his hands and knees before the other had regained his

71

balance. The next assault was a straight lunge aimed at Zen's chest, which he parried at the cost of slit knuckles, then rose to his feet, using his assailant's impetus to throw him clear and to one side.

They were both standing now. Taking the initiative, Zen moved in and aimed a kick at the hand holding the knife, following up with the heel of his right hand slammed up into the man's jaw. He felt completely fearless, even when the swung blade returning stung him on the shoulder. Off balance but totally in control, he stripped the man's shin with the instep of his left foot, causing a satisfying shriek, then stepped back to consider his next move.

It was only then that he noticed the siren and the flashing lights at the far end of the street. A moment later a white Volvo with blue and red stripes and a yellow shield on the door pulled up. Disconcerted, Zen looked round for his attacker. He was nowhere to be seen. Two uniformed patrolmen got out of the car. One of them spoke to Zen, who shrugged and replied in Italian, 'Sorry, I don't understand.' One policeman inspected Zen's hand, which was covered in blood. The other bent down and picked up a knife from the pavement. He got out his radio and made a call, then the two men led Zen over to their car.

The next hour and a half was spent in the emergency department of a hospital, where the injuries to Zen's hand and shoulder were cleaned and the former stitched. At a certain point he remembered the consul's card and the receipt with his address, which he handed to the hospital staff. When Snæbjörn Guðmundsson showed up in person, he initially seemed more agitated by Zen's lack of agitation than by what had actually happened. Zen just ignored him. He was feeling better than he had for months. He had no idea what had happened, still less why. That didn't matter. Something had, and he had dealt with it. He was in charge again, engaged with the real world, making and breaking. It felt good, and he wasn't going to let some weedy, neurotic diplomat tell him otherwise. In fact it was only with the greatest difficulty that Guðmundsson managed to convince Zen to come home with him and go to bed rather than take to the streets and see if there were any bars still open, but in the end he prevailed. They drove somewhere, Zen got out, they went inside, there was a bed, he lay down.

He awoke in a bright, hard light. His shoulder and hand ached abominably, but neither could begin to match his head. He was lying fully clothed on a narrow wooden bed in a musty room filled with cardboard boxes. He had no idea where he was, or any memory of how he got there. The world was a painful enigma whose solution, if there was one, eluded him utterly.

Some time later, Snæbjörn Guðmundsson appeared with a cup of tea in his hand.

'Feeling better?' he asked in an excessively loud and patronizingly cheery tone. 'Bathroom's to the left. I'll be next door when you're ready to talk.'

Twenty minutes later, Zen shambled into the room next door. It was a bleakly austere space stretching from one end of the small one-storey house to the other. The walls were white, the floor bare wooden boards, the furnishings hard and minimal. Since the front door was at one end, he must have crossed the room to get to the bed where he had woken up, but he had absolutely no memory of this.

'So how are you feeling?' Snæbjörn Guðmundsson demanded, putting down the book he had been reading.

'Like hell,' Zen replied succinctly.

'Yes, well, you seemed a bit the worse for wear last night, I have to say. Apart from your various injuries, I mean.'

'I drank a lot.'

'Expensive business here in Iceland.'

'I'll pay you back.'

'Oh, don't worry about that. You're evidently a VIP. I'll bill the embassy.'

Zen collapsed in a chair made of wooden slats on a stainless steel frame. It was as uncomfortable as it looked.

'Did they find the person who attacked me?' he asked.

Guðmundsson looked at him oddly.

'No, they didn't. You say he was dark, unkempt-looking and short?'

'Shorter than me, and I'm shorter than most people here.'

'That's very unusual. Our genetic pool here in Iceland is remarkably homogeneous. Or to put it another way, everyone's related to everyone else. We don't have a distinct class of shorter, dark-skinned people, like the Lapps in Finland.'

'They must be immigrants.'

'That's not really a problem here. We're an island, of course, which helps. The points of entry are strictly controlled and we're very particular about who we let in. Excessively so, some might say, especially if it's a matter of non-Northern European individuals. When the United States military applied to build Keflavik as a base during the war, the government agreed on condition that no black servicemen be stationed there.'

Zen waved dismissively.

'Well, all I know is that I saw plenty of these people about last night. And this was before I got drunk. Like that one I told you I saw standing beside you outside the café yesterday, while you were talking on the phone. They looked different, they dressed different and they acted different. And one of them tried to kill me.'

An odd look came into Guðmundsson's eyes.

'You say they dressed differently. How?'

Zen shrugged.

'I don't know. Like people who had just arrived from some remote village in the country. They were wearing coarse, homespun garments, badly cut and badly put together. They looked completely out of place, like the gypsies in Italy, but it didn't seem to bother them. On the contrary, they were staring at the other people in a really blatant way, with this sort of mocking, malicious smile.'

Snæbjörn Guðmundsson nodded slowly, considering all this. Then he stood up and beckoned.

'Come this way a moment.'

He walked over to the front door and opened it on to the tiny patch of garden that divided the house from the street. The consul looked both ways, then turned to Zen.

'How many people are there in sight at the moment?'

Zen counted rapidly.

'Eleven,' he replied.

'Ah,' said Guðmundsson.

'Why?'

The consul ushered him back inside and closed the door.

'The reason why the police were on the scene so quickly last night was that all of downtown Reykjavík is monitored by a system of closed-circuit video cameras connected to viewing screens at the central police station, to deter and control violence among the roving packs of drunken youths who often go on revelling until five or six in the morning at this time of year. The patrol cars are parked strategically around the perimeter of the area, and can reach any trouble spot in seconds.'

Zen took out his cigarettes and looked questioningly at his host, who nodded.

'The street in which you claim to have been attacked . . .'

'What do you mean, "claim"? Look at my hand! Why do you think I needed all these stitches?'

'Let's leave that for a moment. At all events, the street is not very well lit, and the nearest camera was quite a long way from where this happened. Nevertheless, one of the police officers on duty saw you fall over and then start lashing out with your feet and fists, and called in a patrol car. What he didn't see, and what re-examination of the video tape has failed to reveal, is any evidence of a second person.'

'Are you calling me a liar?' demanded Zen, really angry now.

'Not at all. I'm merely telling you what the police report stated.'

'You think my idea of a good time is to get so drunk I see people who aren't there and then slash my hand and shoulder with a knife I brought along for the purpose?'

'Are you drunk now?' asked the consul.

'No! Just horribly hung over.'

'Of course. Just a moment.'

He walked out to the kitchen, returning a moment later with a small glass filled with a brownish liquid.

'Drink this.'

'What is it?' Zen asked, sniffing the liquid. It smelt indescribably foul.

'Just drink it. Knock it back in one. You'll feel much better.'

Zen did as he was told. A sharp burning sensation in his mouth and throat was abruptly followed by the most intense onrush of nausea he had ever experienced. He knew without the slightest doubt that he was going to vomit massively there and then, all over the consul's hardwood floor. Then it passed, and was succeeded by a warm glow. The consul nodded.

'It's an infusion of *hakarl*, decomposed shark's meat pickled in raw alcohol. In about five minutes you'll feel much better. But it was important to check whether you were still suffering the active effects of the drinks you had last night before evaluating the results of my little test.'

'What test?'

'When I asked how many people there were in the street.'

'I told you, there were eleven.'

Snæbjörn Guðmundsson regarded him solemnly.

'I only saw eight,' he said.

Zen laughed harshly, getting some of his own back at last.

'Maybe you need glasses!'

'There are no glasses made for this.'

'For what?'

Guðmundsson sighed.

'We call it *fylgja*. It's a special faculty. People who have it are called *skyggn*. All children are *skyggn* until they're about five, and many after that. Almost all lose it when they reach puberty, but a few people retain the gift into adult life. It appears that you may be one of them, Dottor Zen. If so, you are only the second foreigner I've ever heard of with this faculty.'

'I have no idea what you're talking about.'

The consul laughed.

'And when I tell you, you're going to think that *I'm* drunk. But try and accept that this is a well-attested phenomenon. What it means, of course, is another matter. It's like talking about religion. You may believe in God or you may not, but it's a perfectly respectable intellectual position to hold that God does not exist and that religion is simply a tissue of meretricious falsehoods designed to give people an illusory sense of purpose. What is not a respectable intellectual position is to hold that people do not have religious experiences. You follow me?'

'What's all this got to do with whatever it is you said I had or was?'

'It's completely analogous. Some people believe in the existence of the *huldufolk*, others don't. Their existence is therefore debatable. What is not debatable is that there are people who claim to be able to see them.'

'See who, for God's sake?'

'The "hidden people". Traditionally, they have been regarded as a race of supernatural beings who live all around us, but in a parallel dimension which is only perceptible to those who are *skyggn*.'

'But you surely don't believe in this nonsense, do you?'

Snæbjörn Guðmundsson shrugged.

'I don't have *fylgja*, so it's all rather theoretical. I'm simply trying to come up with a rational explanation for what happened to you last night, the people you saw in the street, and the one you say attacked you.'

'A rational explanation based on totally irrational premises. If the police camera didn't pick him up, it's because he was dark skinned and wearing dark clothing, that's all.'

The consul laughed.

'Iceland is an odd place, *dottore*. Geologically, it's the youngest landmass on the planet. Think of it as the pizza country. It's about the same shape, and hot out of the oven. Up north they have geysers, volcanoes, lava flows. You can stand there and watch the terrible process of the earth being made, right in front of your eyes, while across the fjord the glaciers are calving icebergs. But enough of all this abstruse talk. How about some lunch?'

Zen shivered visibly.

'I couldn't eat a thing.'

And he meant it. He was hungry, but not for anything you could get here. He needed food for his soul. He needed to go home, before he crossed to the other side of the shadow line

77

Snæbjörn Guðmundsson had described, and became one of the *huldufolk* himself, an invisible alien haunting the streets of this unreal city where it was always midday on the thirtieth of February.

'I think I'll go and lie down for a bit,' he said. 'I didn't sleep well last night.'

Guðmundsson nodded.

'Of course. I'll let you know if there are any developments.'

He was awakened by a light tapping at the door. It opened to reveal the consul.

'You have a visitor,' he said.

Zen rolled up off the bed. It was like being back in hospital, he thought. People came in and out of your room and told you what to do next. He had been living like this for almost a year now. When would he sleep in his own bed again? But where was that bed? Rome, he supposed, but the idea didn't carry complete conviction.

His visitor turned out to be þórunn Sigurðardòttir, the policewoman who had interviewed him at the airport the day before. She nodded at him and made a short speech which Snæbjörn Guðmundsson translated.

'She brings good news. The chief pathologist has now confirmed the preliminary findings of the autopsy performed yesterday. His conclusion is that Signor Angelo Porri died of natural causes, a heart attack to be precise. The police therefore have no further interest in the matter, and you are free to go, with apologies for the unavoidable delay.'

Inspector Sigurðardòttir handed over the passport in the name of Pier Giorgio Butani to Zen. Then she flashed Zen a brief smile, like a shaft of sunlight glancing off an ice field, and left.

'Well, that's all very well,' Zen said testily to Snæbjörn Guðmundsson. 'I can leave, but how? The only ticket I've got is on Alitalia. Do they fly to Iceland?'

'No.'

'Then what am I supposed to do, have them divert another plane to pick me up?'

'I imagine that they will have made arrangements with

another airline to fly you to America. We can check with the airport. But the first step is to inform the embassy in Copenhagen. I'll do that on the land line in my study.'

He returned a few minutes later.

'Well, that's done. They're going to contact Rome. We're to await instructions.'

A silence fell.

'Where did you learn Italian?' asked Zen.

'When I was a student in Florence, many years ago.'

'Studying what?'

'Art.'

'Oh yes, you said you were an artist.'

'Yes.'

Zen glanced around the stridently bare walls.

'So you sell all your work?'

'None of it.'

'None?'

'No. It's no good, you see.'

Zen smiled politely.

'I'm sure you're just being modest.'

'Not at all. I may not be much of an artist, but I'm an excellent judge of art. I sometimes wish I weren't. It might make it possible to believe that my stuff had some value. But it doesn't. I know that.'

'But you keep working?'

'Oh yes. What else would I do?'

'So where are your paintings?'

Snæbjörn Guðmundsson stood up.

'Would you like to see them?'

Zen's heart sank. The last thing he wanted was a guided tour round some amateur dauber's studio. Fortunately the telephone rang next door.

'It's Rome,' said the consul, reappearing in the doorway a moment later. 'For you.'

Guðmundsson's study, by contrast with the living area, was a jumble of papers and files. Zen seated himself at the desk and picked up the phone.

'*Pronto.*'

79

'*Buona sera, dottore.* This is not a secure line, so it's important that we do not identify ourselves or be too specific about the matters under discussion.'

'I understand.'

'We have spoken before, most recently on your connecting flight from Pisa to Milan.'

'Ah yes.'

'I understand that you have had a tiresome time recently, but that everything is now sorted out.'

'That's right. What's not clear is how I'm to continue my journey.'

'The answer is that you aren't.'

'I'm not?'

'No. There have been developments. In fact we have reason to suppose that they may have predated your departure, but our American counterparts have only just seen fit to inform us.'

'I hope there's no lack of trust implied.'

'If so, it would be totally unjustified. There have been no breaches of security this end, I can assure you.'

'That's good to know. So if one of these attempts on my life finally succeeds, I can die secure in the knowledge that the leak was of non-Italian origin.'

'Please don't be facetious. It's also most inappropriate to mention such matters on this connection. In any case, there will be no more such episodes.'

'That's certain, is it?'

'Absolutely certain. As I said, there have been developments, as a result of which the event at which you were to participate in the United States has now been postponed and may well be cancelled altogether.'

Zen hardly dared to believe what he had heard.

'In short, one of the two principal protagonists has decided to co-operate with our side,' the Foreign Ministry man went on. 'As a result, your participation has been rendered superfluous. There is therefore no need for you to attend, and no risk that any further attempts will be made to prevent you from doing so.'

Zen laughed lightly.

'It was Nello, right?' he said.

'Please!'

'All right, but it was, wasn't it?'

'Well, yes. How did you know?'

'He talked to me in the car, while they were driving me to meet you know who. He explained how they lit the landing strip for the aircraft. The other man told him to shut up. I could tell he was a talker then. Any competent cop or magistrate could have got him to open up eventually. He was one of those people who just can't bear to be silent.'

'Well, that's what happened. And you'll be pleased to know that there's some evidence that the incident at Versilia may have been a contributing factor. In their view, it seems, that was their last hope of preventing your appearance at the event in America, and when it failed the outcome was preordained. So one of the protagonists, the one you mentioned, apparently decided to make a deal. His cooperation in return for a new identity and a new life over there.'

'Any chance of that for me?'

'Better still, you can have your old one back. You're to return immediately for a complete briefing at your normal place of employment. Our embassy in Copenhagen will send full details to the consul shortly. I wish you a pleasant journey and a safe return home.'

When Zen reappeared in the living room, Snæbjörn Guð-mundsson looked at him curiously.

'The embassy in Denmark is going to contact you about my travel arrangements,' Zen told him.

'Ah.'

'Basically, I'm going back to Italy.'

'I see.'

'Immediately.'

The consul nodded his understanding of the rules of this game. He glanced at his watch.

'Well, that'll probably be the two-thirty to Copenhagen.'

Zen looked surprised.

'What time is it now?'

'Half past ten. Plenty of time.'

'It can't be only half past ten! It must be noon at least.'

'No, half past ten in the evening. The flight's in the early morning. We're so remote, you see. It takes three hours to get to Europe, and we're on British time, so that's another hour. If you want to get to a business meeting on time, you have to leave after midnight. But don't worry, I'll get you there in plenty of time.'

He looked at Zen and smiled.

'You asked to see my paintings. Come this way.'

Zen, who had completely forgotten this aspect of their conversation, followed the consul into his kitchen, then out into the back yard of the house, a concreted rectangle containing a large pile of black ash.

'There they are,' said Guðmundsson. 'The most recent ones, that is. The others are feeding the flowers in the beds at the front. What do you think?'

Zen gave a nervous smile.

'Are you some sort of performance artist?' he asked.

He had heard of people like that, who did things associated to his mind with circus performers and children's entertainers.

'Well, maybe I am,' Guðmundsson replied. 'I hadn't thought of it that way. This business has disrupted my normal schedule, of course, but on the whole I work hard, six hours a day at least. And at the time I'm always convinced that I've finally managed to produce something worthwhile. But then when it's finished I look at it and realize that I was wrong. It's just another botched job, one more piece of ugly nonsense. And God knows there's enough ugly nonsense in the world already. So I bring it out here and burn it.'

Zen gave what he hoped would be perceived as a judicious nod.

'It's like the Hippocratic Oath,' the consul went on with a face as straight as a priest's. 'All would-be artists should be made to sign it. Rule number one, "Do No Harm". If I can't achieve something even vaguely resembling the sort of art I saw every day while I lived in Italy, the very least I can do is not clutter up the planet with any more trendy bric-a-brac. It seems that all I can manage is the clever, and who needs that? We're all clever these days. We're all so fucking clever. I'd rather make a nice bonfire and at least feel clean afterwards.'

He closed the door and led the way back inside.

'I'd better call the embassy in Copenhagen and find out about your flights.'

Zen went back to the storeroom where he had spent the night, and packed up his bags. When he reappeared next door, Guðmundsson was already there.

'Right. They've booked you on the two-thirty to Copenhagen, as I thought, with an onward connection to Rome. You're to contact someone named Brugnoli on arrival. The tickets will be waiting at the SAS counter at Keflavik. If you're all set, we might as well go.'

Zen lugged his bags back to the car and they set off. As soon as they were past the outskirts of the bleak, cheerless town, Zen felt his spirits rise. He still felt half drunk and totally disorientated, and had had no time to work out the implications of what had happened. But all that mattered was that he was leaving. He had never felt such a visceral urgency to get away from any place.

Suddenly the car drew in to the side of the highway.

'Do you see that rock over there?' asked the consul, pointing.

It was a massive outcropping of volcanic basalt, worn and weathered by the elements into myriad fantastic gullies and crevices.

'That's where they're supposed to live, in rocks like that one, hidden away in the crannies and crevasses. Allegedly they can be very vindictive if disturbed.'

Zen glanced at the consul, who restarted the car and drove on.

'The *huldufolk*, I mean,' he explained. 'There's a rock much like that on the property where my family's summer house is. My father was a member of parliament for the *Alþýðuflokkurinn*, a very radical, left-wing party. He was also a close friend of Halldor Laxness, our Nobel Prize–winning writer, and generally prided himself on being a progressive, forward-looking individual. But when we had a new driveway put in to the summer house, he made the builders go all the way round that rock rather than blow it up, even though it added almost half a kilometre to the length of the drive, and of course to the cost. "You surely don't believe in that superstitious nonsense?" I asked him mockingly. I've never forgotten his reply. "Of course not," he said. "But you can't be too careful."'

They drove on for a while in silence. At last the structures of the airport appeared in the distance. Zen lit a cigarette and turned to Guðmundsson.

'You said that I was only the second case you've heard of where a foreigner had this . . .'

'Fylgja. Yes.'

'Who was the other?'

Guðmundsson laughed.

'It's a droll story. I told you that Keflavik was originally built as a military base during the Second World War. Well, one of the servicemen stationed there started showing symptoms of the condition, going on about people that no one else could see and so on. A lot of those rocks were torn up and blown apart to lay out the runways and base facilities, and so many of the "hidden people" must have been made homeless. At any rate, the medics who examined the man had never heard of the *huldufolk*, of course. They decided the guy was crazy and shipped him back to the States. This was just before the Normandy landings.'

Zen smiled.

'Lucky man!'

'Not really. The ship he was on got torpedoed by a U-boat off Newfoundland and went down with all hands.'

The parking lot at the airport was almost empty. Snæbjörn Guðmundsson pulled up right in front of the handsomely sterile terminal building.

'Now before we part,' he said, turning to Zen, 'I would suggest that you bear in mind what happened to that GI.'

Zen frowned.

'How do you mean?'

Guðmundsson sighed.

'I absolutely believe everything that you told me about what happened to you last night. I also give you my word that I shall not reveal it to anyone else. I strongly advise you to do the same. What may seem quite plausible here in Iceland will sound like arrant lunacy back in Italy. People will remember that car accident you had, and begin to wonder if the injuries you sustained were purely physical. Do you see what I mean?'

Zen nodded.

'Yes, yes. Of course. I thought you meant something else.'

'What?'

'When you said I should bear in mind what happened to the American. I thought you meant that my seeming good luck might turn out to be a death sentence in disguise too.'

Snæbjörn Guðmundsson laughed.

'Of course not! Actually, he was very much the exception. Most people who are *skyggn* enjoy excellent health and live to an exceptionally old age.'

They both got out of the car. The consul fetched a trolley for Zen's bags. Once they were loaded, the two men stood there awkwardly.

'Thank you for your help,' said Zen. 'And good luck with the painting.'

Snæbjörn Guðmundsson grimaced.

'Just one authentic piece before I die, that's all I ask. It doesn't matter how small or insignificant, still less whether anyone else notices or cares. Just one true thing, so that I can feel that my life hasn't been wholly wasted.'

They shook hands.

'It's been a pleasure to meet you, whoever you may be,' Snæbjörn Guðmundsson commented with an arch smile. 'I wish you a safe and pleasant onward journey. And please try and forget about what we've been discussing. It's really just a strictly local folk myth of no wider significance. It may or may not be true here, but it certainly isn't anywhere else. There are no hidden people where you're going!'

ROMA

The first thing he did, after being flushed out of the side entrance of the Stazione Termini in a party of hearty young foreign backpackers and their parasitical horde of touts, rogue cabbies, beggars and pickpockets, was to get something to eat. Not that he had any excuse for feeling hungry. They'd fed him something called 'breakfast' on the flight to Denmark, and something else called 'a snack' on the connecting plane to Fiumicino. But this wasn't a question of physical hunger. His needs were deeper and more complex than that, and luckily he knew just how to satisfy them.

He crossed the busy street, delighting in several near misses and a very ripe insult from one of the drivers vying for position, then headed towards Piazza della Repubblica. After a few more life-enhancing, near-death traffic experiences, he turned left along Via Viminale, humming a sprightly melody he eventually identified as the national anthem, last heard in truncated electronic form emanating from Snæbjörn Guðmundsson's cellphone. 'L'Italia chiamò, stringiamoci a coorte, siam pronti alla morte...'

Opposite a curvaceous section of a redbrick rotunda, once the southern corner of a vast complex of public baths erected by some Roman emperor, stood a poky little establishment about the size of a neighbourhood barber's shop. Inside the window, a roast piglet reclined languidly in a glass case as though taking an afternoon nap. Once through the doorway, there were a few rough wooden tables, chairs and benches. The patron, Ernesto, a short man who had come to closely resemble the product he sold, presided from a zinc serving bar at the back. He gave a mock start of astonishment as Zen walked in.

'I thought you were dead!' he exclaimed in a Roman accent that would have needed one of his own knives to cut.

Zen nodded.

'There was a rumour to that effect.'

The two men shook hands, the owner having wiped his off on his filthy apron.

'That shocking business in Sicily!' exclaimed Ernesto with a massive shrug which effectively erased that island from the atlas. 'It was all over the TV and papers, but of course De Angelis and the rest of the lads gave me the inside story. It's sickening, just sickening! What are we supposed to do with those people? We've tried everything, and nothing works. Let's face it, they're just not like us. Never were, never will be. And now they're talking about building that bridge to the mainland, at the taxpayers' expense, needless to say. You know what I say? Forget it! Stop the ferries! Patrol the straits with gunboats and shoot the bastards if they try to smuggle themselves into the country. They're worse than the Albanians.'

At any other time, Zen might have been inclined to agree, but in his present state he felt like gripping Ernesto by the arms and trying to convince him that they were all – yes, even the Sicilians – *fratelli d'Italia*. He had enough common sense left, though, to realize that this would not do. Although open to the general public, Ernesto's establishment also functioned as a private club for a circle of privileged regulars, and like any club it had its rules. One of these was that a certain amount of purely rhetorical racism had to be tolerated in the spirit in which it was offered, as an innocuous way of establishing commonality and bonding, expressing solidarity and exasperation, and excluding outsiders. Like the human body, a community could only tolerate a certain degree of invasive otherness without internal collapse. The Romans had had fifteen hundred years of practice in the necessary strategies of passive aggression, and Zen for one did not feel that it was his business to criticize them. The baths which once covered this whole area of the city might have been pillaged and quarried and razed to the ground, but the people were still here.

'So where have you been all this time?' Ernesto went on.

'They told us you'd survived that Mafia bomb, but when you didn't show up here I began to wonder. Maybe they're not telling us the truth, I thought. Even De Angelis didn't seem to know anything definite. Maybe we're all out of the loop, I thought. Maybe the whole thing is just a huge lie! After all, it wouldn't be the first time, would it?'

Zen seated himself at one of the narrow tables.

'It certainly wouldn't.'

'So where were you?'

'At the end of the earth, Ernesto. It's a long story, and I've got an appointment at the office in fifteen minutes. Meanwhile I'm ready for some real food.'

'Right away, *dottore*! The usual?'

'The usual.'

Ernesto took one of the filled rolls from the glass cabinet, set it on a plate, then added two more thick slices from the roast and set it down in front of Zen along with a small carafe of white wine and a knife and fork.

'I carved it extra fatty,' he said with a conspiratorial wink. 'You're looking a bit peaky, *dottore*. We'll have to feed you up.'

Zen cut a chunk of the pale, perfumed meat and started to chew. Apart from wine, Ernesto only served one thing: *porchetta*, choice young piglets from farmers personally known to him, stuffed with fennel and herbs, slowly roasted to moist perfection on a spit and served cold with chewy fresh bread. The crackling was a crisp layer of rich delights, the fat a creamy, unctuous decadence, the flesh tender and aromatic. Even the generic Castelli Romani wine, which couldn't have been given away free as a household cleanser in Venice, tasted blandly acceptable to Zen today.

As he turned his attention to the roll, having satisfied his immediate craving for flavourful protein, he began to wonder what lay ahead in his imminent interview at the Ministry just down the street. The name Brugnoli meant nothing to him, but this in itself was not surprising. Zen had been out of commission and away from his desk for almost a year, and in Italian politics a year is a very long time. Indeed, he had heard rumours that in his absence there had been yet another general election. But while the players might have changed, the game was likely to remain fairly predictable. The Craxis and Andreottis might be either dead or in retirement, just like their erstwhile enemies, the hard men of the Red Brigades, but to this day no one knew for sure how Aldo Moro had been kidnapped with such breathtaking ease and efficiency, nor why he had been killed. It was like Argentina after the collapse of the military dictatorship. The old regime had been swept away, but a general amnesty and a still more general collective amnesia were in effect.

The implications for Zen's career were not positive. From what the Foreign Ministry official had told him in coded euphemisms on the phone, the case against Nello and Giulio Rizzo, if it ever came to court, could be resolved without Zen's testimony. That removed any further threat to his life from Mafia hit men, but it also removed any interest that the Italian authorities might have had in him. The early retirement which had been hinted at back when he was still convalescing now beckoned. There would be polite speeches, perhaps even a few perks in the way of his pensionable grade and so on, but basically he would be out. At the very best, they might kick him upstairs to a position as Questore at some sleepy provincial police headquarters where he would shuffle files, oversee routine administrative work and generally watch the clock until he was eased out altogether.

But what he needed was work, and more urgently than ever before. He had never felt particularly zealous or committed to his job until now, when it was in danger of being taken away from him along with his mother, his adopted daughter and a whole way of life he had casually taken for granted, as though it would always be there. Now that it looked like it very well might not be, he asked himself in a sort of panic what he was to do. He would have enough money to live on comfortably, but how was he going to get through the day? What would he do at nine o'clock and noon and six in the evening, and why? What would be the point of it all?

He wiped his mouth on the paper napkin, paid the modest bill, assured Ernesto of his satisfaction and continued custom in the future, and continued down the street to the café at the next corner, where he downed an espresso and smoked a cigarette which tasted as acrid as the one traditionally offered to the condemned man.

The guard at the gate of the Interior Ministry building did not recognize Zen, but after some discussion allowed him to proceed as far as the security checkpoint at the main entrance. The plain-clothed functionary who presided here was a big man with squidgy features, clumsy gestures and the embittered air of someone painfully coming to terms with the fact that his boyhood dream of some day becoming a small-time pimp in Centocelle had probably passed him by.

He demanded to see identification. Zen explained that he had been working undercover and was not carrying any. The failed pimp retorted that no one got in without identification, in a tone suggesting that the very fact that Zen had been unaware of this already made him a potential suspect.

'I have an appointment with someone named Brugnoli,' said Zen. 'Does the name ring a bell?'

'We don't disclose the identity of Ministry personnel.'

'Well, can you call him and let him know I'm here?'

The man jerked a thumb over his shoulder.

'The phone's at the main desk.'

Zen started forward, and was immediately restrained by an outstretched hand.

'I can't let you in without valid identification.'

The official's tone of voice indicated clearly that there was no point in trying to reason with him. Zen turned away, walked down the steps into the courtyard of the building and dialled a number on his mobile phone. A voice he didn't recognize answered.

'Sì.'

'C'è De Angelis?'

'Un momentino.'

The voice receded, calling out, 'Giorgio! For you.' After a further pause, Giorgio De Angelis came on the line.

'Well?' he said bad-temperedly.

'Ciao, Giorgio. Sono Aurelio.'

There was a pause, then a deafening cry.

'Aurelio! How are you? Where are you?'

'Standing outside the front door to the building. I don't have my ID and the security guard won't let me in. Can you persuade him of the error of his ways?'

'I'll be right down.'

Zen was smoking another cigarette when De Angelis appeared outside the doorway and bounded down to embrace his friend.

'How wonderful to see you looking so well!' he exclaimed.

'It's good to be back. I don't know how long for, though.'

'But what are you doing here? I thought you were off for a working holiday in the States.'

Zen immediately took a certain distance.

'You're not supposed to know that,' he said. 'No one is.'

De Angelis shrugged.

'It's just something someone said. You know how it is. I had no idea whether it was true or not.'

'But you passed it on to a few other people anyway.'

'Only a couple. What happened to your hand?'

'I had an accident with a knife.'

'Are you free for lunch?'

'I've already eaten. Plus I have an appointment with someone called Brugnoli, whoever he may be.'

De Angelis rolled his eyes.

'Ah, our new "facilitator".'

'What's that supposed to mean?'

'You'll see.'

At the security checkpoint, De Angelis showed his badge and obtained a temporary pass for Zen on his own recognizance.

'Top floor, naturally,' he said. 'If you feel like talking afterwards, I'll be at the Opera.'

He inclined his head steeply backwards, seemingly inspecting the mock cupola above their heads as though for signs of earthquake damage.

'I mean really talking,' he added.

Brugnoli's office was the second on the left of the 'good' side of the top floor, the one with the view of the Quirinale. There was no sign on the door or beside it, but Zen had been assured by some young men hunched over computer screens in another room he had entered at random that this was the right place. There had been no identifying sign on their door, either.

The reception area inside the unmarked door was unlike anything Zen had ever seen at the Viminale. There was a leather sofa and matching armchairs, a low table covered in magazines and art books, a number of large potted plants with fleshy outsized leaves, a printed sign thanking Zen for not smoking, and a large video screen showing current stock prices on various international markets. In the opposite corner, next to an imposing internal door, a faux blonde in a pink lambswool twinset was picking fussily at a computer. The walls were painted a genteel pastel shade of peach and the Persian rug underneath the low table looked too threadbare and faded to be anything but a genuine antique. Gentle classical music made itself felt at a barely subliminal level, while recessed halogen lamps diffused a clear, restrained light on a space that had either nothing or everything to hide. It looked less like the antechamber to the lair of a high-ranking Ministry official than the premises of a dentist whose bill would prove to be even more painful than the treatment.

Zen introduced himself to the receptionist. She touched her computer screen in three places, like a priest blessing a communicant. A moment later, the inner door opened and a short, energetic man with receding hair and a jovial smile emerged.

'Dottor Zen! What a pleasure! You've had a smooth trip, I hope? The way back always seems shorter and sweeter than the way out, I find.'

He caught Zen staring slack-jawed at his open-necked shirt, stonewashed jeans and black running shoes.

'Dress-down Friday,' he explained. 'One of my little innovations around here. It has encountered a certain amount of resistance from some of the older team members, I'm afraid, but of course I don't insist. That's my whole philosophy of the workplace environment. "Personal choice, personal empowerment, personal responsibility." All that counts is results. Come in, come in!'

Zen followed Brugnoli through the doorway, feeling like a

superannuated bank clerk in his fifteen-year-old suit, a shirt that felt as though it consisted mostly of starch, and shoes of the now extinct variety that could be and indeed had been resoled.

The room they entered was completely different from the reception area outside, but just as much of a surprise. It was about the same size and height as the entire upper floor of the Rutelli family's villa in Versilia, but looked as though it had been redecorated by Snæbjörn Guðmundsson. The floor was tiled, the walls studiously bare and neutral. A minimalist desk in some synthetic black material supported a flat-screen computer terminal and nothing else. No telephone, no drawers, no paperwork. There were no filing cabinets in evidence either, nor any of the usual bookshelves groaning under a weight of identically bound legal tomes. No portrait of the current occupant of the Quirinale Palace visible though the floor-length windows, no crucifixes or flags, no framed documents in cursive script certifying that Dottor Brugnoli had been the recipient of this or that honour or award. In fact the only other objects on view in the huge space were a terracotta bust of a man's head, mounted on an exiguous metal stand which seemed to be performing a balancing act like a juggler on a high wire, and a framed Fascist-era poster showing two men in uniform chatting in the street while a sinister eavesdropper lurked in the shadows. 'Be Vigilant!' warned the caption in mock three-dimensional characters. 'Walls Have Ears.'

So this was what it had come to, thought Zen glumly. The received but always unspoken wisdom of his professional generation had now been recycled as public postmodern irony. It was definitely time for him to quit.

Meanwhile his host had retreated to the far corner of the room, where he was walking up and down talking intensely to himself. By now familiar with this epidemic which had recently started to afflict large numbers of the population, Zen turned politely away, pretending not to notice. That seemed to be the form. You'd be walking along the street, and this well-dressed and apparently successful man would come at you, head up and briefcase in hand, talking to himself. Sometimes even arguing with himself in a loud and insistent voice. It was as if all the drunks and schizos had been given million-lire clothing allowances and a middle-management job. Except that just as in the old days, when they lay in piss-stained doorways mumbling obscenities or screaming abuse, no one took the slightest notice. 'Pay no attention, he's harmless,' he recalled his mother telling him as a child in Venice about some veteran of the Great War whose mind had slipped its moorings. 'Just don't ever turn your back on them, that's all. Don't look them in the eye and never turn your back.'

He froze, frowning at some unrecovered thought. The gist of it was that he had ignored his mother's advice. That there was someone into whose eyes he had looked, and on whom he had then turned his back. One of 'them'. But that was as far as the insight went, and it made no sense.

Brugnoli terminated his conversation with a curt, 'It'll have to wait, I've got someone with me', then adjusted the microphone of his headset and turned back to Zen with a convivial smile.

'Can't offer you a chair, I'm afraid. I don't go in for that sort of thing. You know, the low chair, the high chair, the big desk, the status symbols and hierarchical markers. If you need that sort of nonsense to proclaim and bolster your standing, then you haven't got any. Besides, standing is more natural and more productive. Keeps oxygen flowing to the brain instead of the bum, don't you think?'

'I suppose so.'

'But of course I was forgetting your injuries! How thoughtless of me. Feel free to use the stool by the desk if you wish. It's a revolutionary design. You sort of kneel down into it. Works wonders for the spine and circulation.'

'I'm fine, thank you.'

'Completely?'

'More or less. I still get the odd twinge, but the doctors say that will pass. Apart from that, I'm back to normal.'

Brugnoli gave a pleased smile.

'Excellent! In that case, *dottore*, I can give you some rather good news.'

He stood poised, his face densely pensive, as though posing for a news photographer.

'I have been thinking for some time,' he said, 'of setting up a rather special unit within Criminalpol, and I would like to take this opportunity of inviting you to become its founding member.'

Zen said nothing. Brugnoli swung round with a dramatic, self-deprecating gesture.

'No, "unit" isn't the right word. You'll have to forgive me, *dottore*. Even I sometimes fall into the old habits of speech. What I have in mind is enabling a team of experienced, dedicated individuals with a proven track record for intelligence, intuition and above all initiative. My own version of the famous "Three I's".'

He smiled wryly for the hypothetical camera.

'Personal initiative, like personal responsibility, is something which I fear has not traditionally been prioritized within this department. But believe me, that is about to change. In the new climate, with the new government, the new culture, the new society in the making, this Ministry is, in the last resort, simply a business organization like any other. We have goals to achieve, issues to address, targets to meet and, most important of all, a vision to implement. The fusty old managerial skills of the past cannot rise to these challenges. We have to start thinking outside the box! We need fresh blood, fresh ideas and a fresh approach.

'Not all our present staff have proved to be responsive to this new outlook, I regret to say. To be perfectly frank, some have been downright hostile. I am therefore currently drawing up a plan for a phased retirement scheme designed to offer such individuals a non-negotiable golden handshake amounting to eighty per cent of the salary they would receive for their remaining years of service. I shall be putting it to the Minister shortly, but I'm happy to say that he has already indicated his agreement in principle. The union also seems favourably disposed, thanks to various peripheral clauses, so there's every chance that within a year or so at the most we'll be able to start cutting away a lot of the dead wood around here – and at a price considerably less than paying them to continue not doing their jobs!'

Brugnoli abruptly dropped the public persona and turned round with a man-to-man expression, as if Zen were a privileged viewer who was being shown the sections of the televised interview that were 'off the record'.

'But we must be careful how we wield the axe. The last thing I want is to deprive this concern of the services of more mature operatives who might well prove to be an invaluable asset as we confront the varying demands for our products and services in the future. Men like you, *dottore*.'

He stared pointedly at Zen, who nodded.

'What would be involved?' he asked cautiously.

'A substantial pay rise, for a start! On a par with Questore level, although I'm glad to say that you won't have that discredited title. One of my long-term goals is to restructure our entire organization, phasing out all those Fascist-era positions associated with authoritarianism, repression and control of territory, and replacing them with more flexible classifications that emphasize the wide-ranging public-service nature of our work. Crime issues today are no longer province-specific, they're national and, increasingly, inter- and supranational. In order to be able to respond effectively, we need to operate on the same level. Needless to say, any attempt to make such changes runs up against entrenched opposition and petty vested interests at every turn, which is why I have decided to start with this relatively modest initiative within Criminalpol itself.'

'But what would I actually do?' Zen replied.

'Very much what you have in the past, but without all the bother of coming into the office to deal with endless meetings, paperwork and routine drudgery. Your time and skills are too valuable to be wasted like that, *dottore*. The whole concept is completely outmoded, a relic left over from the early industrial era, when the factory could only function if all the workers showed up when the whistle blew. Now that we can communicate instantly and securely at any time and in any place, what on earth is the point of someone like you trudging in here every morning to sit at a desk taking phone calls and filing reports? I'm interested in results, not reports. Under the new system, you would save yourself two hours a day commuting all the way in here, not to mention freeing up valuable office space which could be used more productively and profitably. Do you see what I mean?'

I'm starting to get the idea, thought Zen.

'In your case, there will be absolutely no need for you to come to the Ministry at all, except perhaps for a weekly progress meeting with a select group of other senior personnel.'

He laughed.

'A bit like turning up for mass on Sunday. And no one will make a fuss if you miss a week or two, as long as you make a full and frank confession of course! Apart from that you will operate strictly on a case-by-case basis. You will be fully briefed, then given a free hand to proceed as you see fit. Needless to say, you can depend on the full backing of this organization at all times, but there will be no attempt to monitor or control your activities. "Personal choice, personal empowerment, personal responsibility." As I've told you, that's my slogan. But it's not just a slogan, *dottore*, it's a way of life.'

Brugnoli held out his hand to Zen with a vigour which somehow suggested the eagle reaching for Prometheus's liver.

'I want to thank you for your valuable input and collaboration, *dottore*, and to be the first to congratulate you on your promotion to this challenging position. You will naturally need a transitional period to make the necessary arrangements before assuming your new duties, and I'm happy to tell you that the villa in Versilia where you were staying earlier is at your disposition for the remainder of the month. Go back to the beach, relax and recharge. It's been a pleasure doing business with you, and I can't wait to welcome you aboard again just as soon as you are fully recovered.'

Zen gracefully took both the hint and his leave. Outside in reception, the faux blonde called him over to the desk and gave him an envelope.

'You need to pick up some equipment that has been allocated to you,' she said. 'Take this docket down to Supplies.'

It's a gun, thought Zen as he made his way out into the corridor and down the stairs. They're giving me a gun so that I can do the decent thing and shoot myself.

'Supplies' turned out to be the department in the basement which had previously been known simply as the depository, presided over by Tullio Rastrelli, a sour, scrawny *sottufficiale* who had lost his right arm when he ran his patrol car into a train at a level crossing while in hot pursuit of a teenage driver who had made a rude gesture at him. Now, though, the counter was manned by a young woman who alarmed Zen by flashing one of those insincere smiles of the sales clerks you see in television commercials, and then asking in what way she could assist him. Zen handed over the envelope. The woman tore it open and read the contents.

'If you'll be so good as to wait one minute, I'll be right back,' she said with another smile.

'And if I'm not so good, you'll never return?'

She gave him a startled glance.

'Pardon?'

Zen shook his head.

'Never mind.'

The woman walked off along the shelving stacked with weapons, ammunition, handcuffs, batons, shields, helmets, and all the other dismal tools of their brutal trade. Zen thought about other times he had come down here, then decided to stop thinking.

Some time later, the woman returned with a small cardboard box which she placed on the counter.

'If you'd be so good as to sign here,' she said, pointing to the docket.

'Yes?' said Zen.

She looked at him.

'Pardon?'

'What's in the box?'

'Oh, I'd be delighted to demonstrate the various features.'

'If I did what?'

'Pardon?'

'Never mind.'

The woman opened one end of the box and shook out a

black plastic oblong that looked rather like one of the early mobile phones, except that there was no keypad. In its place were three large buttons, one green, one yellow and one red, the last covered by a clear plastic shield. She clicked a further button on the side and the other three glowed with a pale radiance.

'This unit combines functional efficiency with rugged durability and extreme ease of use,' she said in a practised tone. 'As you see, there are just three user options. The green button allows you to respond to an incoming call, the yellow initiates an outgoing call, while the red activates the dedicated alarm. Full range over the entire national territory is ensured by the use of military frequencies and facilities, but the really exciting feature is the GPS function.'

'Excite me.'

The woman smiled nervously.

'A chip in the unit continuously monitors the system of Global Positioning Satellites, and calculates the exact position and height above sea level to within a few metres. When the red button is depressed, that information is automatically encoded along with the distress call and forwarded to headquarters for the use of the designated back-up personnel. The installed cadmium battery lasts for up to seventy-two hours with average use. It's fully charged now, and can be recharged in under an hour with the adaptor pack included. And all this in a unit weighing less than three hundred grams!'

'Do you offer a quantity discount?'

'Pardon?'

'Never mind. So if the phone rings, I press the green button.'

'It doesn't ring, it vibrates.'

'Pardon? No, that's your line.'

'If you keep it in an inside pocket or on your hip, anywhere in contact with your body, you will feel a gentle tingling sensation.'

'That'll be the first time for a while.'

'Pardon?'

'Sorry. You were saying?'

'The reason for this feature is the operative may be in a situation where it is not expedient to reveal the fact that he is in communication with headquarters. In such a case, simply ignore the call and report back in when you are able by pressing the green button.'

She turned the unit off and replaced it in its box.

'Any other questions?'

'What happened to Tullio?' asked Zen, pocketing the box.

'Pardon?'

'Tullio Rastrelli. He used to run this place.'

The woman's face almost imperceptibly glazed over.

'Ah, yes,' she said. 'He took early retirement.'

'When Dottor Brugnoli arrived.'

'That's right. It was probably a wise decision. Like a lot of the older members of staff, he didn't really fit into the new ethos here.'

'I can imagine.'

'Dottor Brugnoli's philosophy is that we should think as individuals but act as a team.'

'And Tullio wasn't a team player.'

'Not really, no.'

Zen nodded.

'Brugnoli's full of new ideas, isn't he?'

The woman's eyes glowed.

'Oh I know! He's just so inspirational. He's even having signs printed up for every workplace with phrases like that one, to help keep the staff motivated and focussed. I'm hoping to get one soon.'

Zen left the cardboard box on the counter and slipped the communication device and adaptor pack into his coat pocket.

'Don't get too motivated,' he said, turning towards the door. 'Brugnoli's ambitious, and this Ministry is a political dead end. Come the next cabinet reshuffle, he'll be gone. But those "older members of staff" you mentioned will still be around.'

Ten minutes later, he walked into the Bar Gran Caffè dell'-Opera. Giorgio De Angelis was sitting at a table by the window.

'Tell me all,' he said as Zen sat down, 'then let's see if we can work out what it really means.'

'I don't think that will be too difficult,' Zen replied sourly.

He gave Giorgio a paraphrased version of what Brugnoli had said, inserting a few of the choicer lines verbatim for comic effect, and they were duly effective.

When he'd stopped laughing, De Angelis said, 'I see you're already fluent in the new dialect, Aurelio.'

'There was just one phrase I didn't understand. Something about "the Three I's".'

'That's their motto for the way forward in this country,' De Angelis retorted in a tone of disgust. ' "*Inglese, impresa, Internet*". This is the new Right, Aurelio. Statism with a human face. Well, with a business suit, anyway. No more canny old spiders like Andreotti spinning their intricate webs. Now it's all feel-good slogans and photo-ops carefully stage-managed by Publitalia. Christ, whoever would have thought that we'd miss the former regime so soon? Listen, if this new job doesn't work out, you're welcome to mine. When this retirement plan they've been threatening us with comes into effect, I'm going to cash in.'

'You don't understand, Giorgio. I can't have your job, or even my old one. That's the whole point.'

De Angelis looked at him, suddenly serious.

'How do you mean?'

'I mean I'm being promoted out of harm's way.'

'They're kicking you upstairs?'

'Upstairs and to the left, all the way down the corridor to that little room at the end where no one ever goes. At least, that's the way I read it.'

'But why?'

'I don't know.'

'What harm could you do them?'

'I have no idea. That's what's so worrying. If they simply wanted to get rid of me, they could have told me to take indefinite sick leave until this retirement deal comes through – the least we could do for *un mutilato di guerra e del lavoro*, etcetera, etcetera – and then handed me a cheque and kissed me goodbye. But for some reason I don't understand, they seem to want to keep me in the organization but not of it, if you see what I mean.'

'Out of touch but under control?'

Zen nodded.

'As I say, I have no idea why, but I can't read it any other way. Can you?'

De Angelis pondered this for some time.

'Maybe you're being too cynical,' he said at last.

'One can never be too cynical.'

'That's pretty cynical. Try to be more positive. Maybe they really do respect your abilities and skills and want to put them to the best possible use.'

Zen fixed him with a glassy eye.

' "To facilitate positive interactions and innovative strategies fostering enhanced productivity in the crime issue resolution sector"? I don't think so, Giorgio.'

He turned to the window beside them.

'Anyway, who cares?' exclaimed De Angelis. 'It sounds like a hell of a deal to me, whatever their motives may be. No staff meetings, no routine paperwork, no supervision and no bullshit? Anyone in Criminalpol would kill for an offer like . . .'

'Giorgio.'

'What?'

'Look out there.'

De Angelis followed Zen's gaze to the street outside.

'What?'

'How many people can you see?'

Giorgio De Angelis attempted a laugh, which did not come off.

'What kind of question is that?' he demanded.

'How many?' insisted Zen, not turning to look at him.

De Angelis sighed.

'One, two, three, four, five. Now four. Now six. Now five again. No, now it's . . .'

'Can you see someone leaning against the wall right opposite, between that blue Fiat and the scooter?'

'That young jerk in the green shirt? Yes, Aurelio, I can. My distance vision is still remarkably good, although I have some difficulty reading small print. Speaking of which, would you mind telling me what this is all about?'

For a moment Zen was tempted to try and explain, but by now he was sane enough to restrain himself.

'Oh, nothing. I just thought I recognized him, that's all.'

De Angelis regarded him with unmitigated perplexity.

'How am I supposed to know whether you recognized him? Anyway, that's not what you said. You asked if I could see him.'

'Yes, I suppose I did. Never mind. Let's just forget it.'

Giorgio De Angelis gave a perfunctory nod.

'Very well. He's gone now anyway. So you're not off to America after all?'

'No. One of the two brothers I was supposed to testify against has apparently worked out a *sistemazione* with the prosecutors.'

'As a result of which they don't need you any more.'

'Exactly.'

'Shame. I was there a few years ago. A private trip to visit relatives in Chicago. You'd have liked it.'

Zen sniffed.

'I've never had any desire to go anywhere that wasn't part of the Roman Empire.'

As soon as the sentence was spoken, he realized how pompous it sounded. De Angelis looked at him in a way that made Zen realize suddenly that their friendship, if not over, had at least shifted in some important way. A moment later, he thought: he's envious.

'But if you'd been around at the time of the Roman Empire,' De Angelis replied, 'where would you have wanted to live? Carthage? Barcelona? Marseilles? London? Byzantium? Antioch? Alexandria? All very nice provincial cities with low crime rates, state-of-the-art amphitheatres and immaculately maintained forums, and regularly topping the list of "Ten Most Livable Cities in the Empire". No, you'd have wanted to live in Rome, at the heart of the beast, where the horrible action was. Well, today America is Rome.'

Zen nodded abstractedly.

'Have you heard about La Biacis?' De Angelis murmured.

The last thing Zen wanted to hear about was Tania Biacis,

yet another former girlfriend who'd toyed with him for a while and then decided she could do better. But it would of course have been fatal to display the least reluctance to hear whatever Giorgio had to say.

'How is she?' he asked.

'Rich,' De Angelis replied. 'And I mean seriously rich. Remember that start-up company she founded to export authentic food and drink from the Friuli? Well, she branched out and started handling other small quality producers in other areas of the country, nearly all in the south. When the Internet came along she saw her chance, hired a firm to design a killer web site, and started selling online. Agrofrul – now branded as Delizie – got big write-ups in a bunch of those glossy food-porn mags, and the next thing you know she was deluged with orders from all over the world. I mean she was shipping Calabrian honey to America and Sicilian *bottarga di tonno* to Japan!'

Zen smiled thinly. He was thinking of his interview with Pórunn Sigurðardóttir, the Icelandic policewoman. Maybe Tania's private *impresa*, which she had used to run from her desk at the Ministry, had been the inspiration for the cover story he had given her. He hadn't thought consciously about Tania for years, though, and certainly didn't want to hear about her now. Nevertheless, he nodded.

'Good for her.'

De Angelis laughed.

'No, no. That's just the set-up. Then she got really smart. Just before the dot.com market crashed, she sold out to a multinational distributor looking for a high-end flagship line.'

'But why would she do that, if the business was so successful?'

De Angelis held up his right hand, the fingers outspread. Zen shrugged impatiently.

'*Cinque miliardi,*' pronounced De Angelis distinctly. 'Five billion lire. She'd already quit her job here, of course. The last I heard, she's bought a fabulous abandoned monastery near her native village in the Friuli and is restoring it as a luxury hotel and resort for the discerning rich.'

Zen nodded vaguely. De Angelis slapped him on the stomach with the back of his hand.

'You should have stuck with her, Aurelio. Then you could have told Brugnoli where to put this McJob he's dreamt up for you.'

He glanced at his watch.

'Well, I must be going.'

'All right. But keep in touch. Come up to Versilia for the weekend some time. I'll be there till the end of the month. Bring the wife and kids too, if you want. There's plenty of room.'

'I might take you up on that.'

'You should.'

The two men shook hands with a certain constraint, and then Zen walked back to the railway station, where he picked up his bags from the left-luggage office and took a cab to his home in the Prati district.

It was as his 'home' that he still thought of it, but the moment he turned the key in the lock and stood on the threshold, he realized that here, too, things had changed. A shaft of sunlight created a rectangle of brilliance on the floor, casting the rest of the room into comparative obscurity. The light looked as still and solid as a marble plinth, and yet it was changing even as he gazed at it. That was the real problem, he thought. The boundary between the darkness and the light was shifting all the time, but too subtly for us to be aware of it, except when it was too late.

He had not been in the apartment for almost a year, and then only to make the necessary arrangements for his mother's funeral. Every horizontal surface was covered in a fine layer of dust, while cobwebs hung like wisplets of high grey cloud from the ceiling. Maria Grazia, the housekeeper and latterly Giuseppina's nurse, had long wanted to retire to her native village, but given the demands of Zen's job and his mother's state of health had loyally agreed on various occasions to stay on 'for the time being'. Following Signora Zen's death, however, she had finally given her notice. Oddly, Zen found himself missing her presence more than he did that of his mother.

He lifted the phone and was greeted by silence. Evidently it had been cut off for non-payment of bills. He walked over to the kitchen door and flicked the light switch. Nothing. Probably the gas and water didn't work either. This bothered him less than the phone being dead. He already felt sufficiently isolated and forgotten, an honorary member of the *huldufolk*.

On instinct, he dug his mobile phone out of his baggage and dialled Gilberto Nieddu.

The number rang and rang. Zen was just about to give up when a voice answered.

'Fuck off,' it said. 'I don't care any more, understand? It's over. Just leave me alone, all right? Is that too much to ask?'

'You're not talking to me, Gilberto,' said Zen.

'Who's this?'

'Aurelio.'

'Who?'

Zen didn't answer. There was a silence.

'Oh. Yes. Hi, Aurelio.'

Well, thought Zen, this is different. Since emerging from his shadow persona as Pier Giorgio Butani, everyone he'd spoken to so far had been all over him with questions and theories and opinions about what had or hadn't happened to him in Sicily and since. Yet here was Gilberto, his closest friend, acting as though Zen had just got back from a week's walking holiday in the Dolomites.

'So who did you think was calling?' Zen asked.

'Oh, it doesn't matter.'

'What are you doing?'

'Drinking.'

'Drinking what?'

'Who cares?'

'Are you all right, Gilberto?'

'No.'

'Why? What's happened?'

'Nothing. It doesn't matter.'

Zen took a deep breath.

'Where are you?'

'At home.'

'Can I come round?'

'Suit yourself.'

'In an hour or two?'

'Whenever.'

'I've been travelling all night and I'm exhausted.'

'So you're not feeling chirpy? Good. I couldn't stand chirpiness.'

'I don't think there's much risk of that.'

Gilberto hung up. Zen followed suit, wishing he hadn't called in the first place. Since leaving the police and setting up on his own account in the security and electronic surveillance business, Nieddu's career had been a roller-coaster ride of success, failure and close brushes with the law. When Zen had last been in touch, enlisting his friend's help in extricating himself from a difficult situation he had found himself in during his posting to Catania, the situation had seemed to be improving. This latest contact seemed to confirm that, once again, the Sardinian had not overlooked an opportunity to plunge himself back into crisis.

Gilberto and his wife Rosa lived in Via Carlo Emanuele, near Porta Maggiore. They owned an apartment in a modern block, which had been borderline affordable when they bought it. By now, it must have been worth a fortune. Zen walked up the gleaming stairs to the first floor and rang the bell. Outside the tall metal-framed windows, it was already dark. He had slept for over three hours.

He had to ring twice before the door opened and a man's face appeared. Unshaven, unfocussed, at once haggard and bloated, it was barely identifiable as that of Gilberto Nieddu.

'Oh, it's you,' he said, throwing the door open so violently that it slammed against the wall, and instantly turning back inside.

Zen followed, closing the door quietly behind him. The smells hit him first, a whole orchestra of them tuning up before the conductor arrived and they unleashed their full power. Once inside, the visual aspect kicked in. The pleasant, bright, orderly apartment Zen remembered had been transformed into an unrecognizable state of squalid disorder and abandon. In the living room, dirty clothes lay across the furniture and floor, an array of empty bottles and used glasses covered the table, and the air was blue with cigarette smoke. The kitchen to the left had piles of dishes and saucepans on every work surface, while still more were stacked high in the sink.

'Well, this is the scene of the crime, Dottor Zen,' Gilberto remarked with arch jocularity, reaching for one of the half-empty glasses. 'What do you make of it?'

Zen coughed apologetically. He did not sit down.

'It looks like Rosa's left you,' he said.

Nieddu laughed.

'Bravo! Nothing can escape the eagle eye and awesome intelligence of the renowned Aurelio Zen. He takes a few seemingly insignificant and unrelated clues overlooked by less astute observers, processes them faster than a supercomputer and lays bare the mystery which had baffled the finest minds of Europe. Yes, the little bitch has left me.'

Zen sighed heavily.

'When?'

'Four days ago? Three? Six? I forget. Who cares? She's gone, that's all that matters. She's gone and she's not coming back. She made that very clear.'

He collapsed on the sofa, grabbed a bottle and poured some colourless spirit into the glass he had been using.

'Very clear indeed,' he added quietly, as though addressing the bottle.

'So where is she now?'

'Back home in Sassari with her younger brother,' Nieddu continued in the same quiet tone, all bravado gone. 'Who is threatening to come over shortly and break my legs.'

'And the children?'

'With her, of course. I came home one day to find the place empty, all their clothes and belongings gone, and a note on the table.'

Zen lit a cigarette.

'What happened?'

'A friend of hers saw me and a member of my staff having dinner at a restaurant down at the beach in Lido di Ostia when I was supposedly in Turin on business. Rosa had had her suspicions about me for years, but this was the first time she'd ever been able to prove anything. Her note gave me to understand that she was taking steps to ensure that it would also be the last.'

Zen nodded.

'So you've been doing this for years and finally got caught.'

Nieddu refilled his glass.

'Want a drink? No? Good idea. Yes, I got caught, and you know why? Because I'd stopped trying so hard. That business in Lido di Ostia, I'd never have risked anything that stupid in the old days. If I said I was going to Turin, I'd go. What happened there was another matter. But you get old, you get lazy. Mobile phones haven't helped, either. Time was, you had to say where you'd be staying and leave the number, but now you could be anywhere.'

He took a large gulp of his drink.

'But that's not really it.'

'So what is?'

Nieddu lit a cigarette and lay down on the sofa.

'She got old, Aurelio. What else can I say? She got old.'

Zen did not reply. After a while, Nieddu leaned over and flicked the ash of his cigarette into his drink.

'You know that saying about generals? That they're always superbly prepared to fight the last war? It's not just generals, it's all of us.'

'I don't understand.'

'Can you imagine if we were twenty again, or even thirty, how easy it would be for us to win at the kind of games people that age play? We'd be unbeatable, not least because we wouldn't care too much if we won, the way we did back then. We were under too much pressure, there was too much at stake. No wonder we fucked up.'

'I still don't see what this has to do with you and Rosa.'

'I thought I was one of those generals. I thought I had the situation all worked out. Basically, I thought I could get away with a certain amount of action on the side, providing I was discreet about it. But that wasn't the real point.'

'So what was?'

'That it was still working for us in bed. Maybe she even did have some proof of what I was getting up to, I don't know, but as long as she was getting her share of attention it didn't bother her that much. But things were changing, like they always do. You don't notice it, any more than you notice the days growing shorter at this time of year. But they are, imperceptibly. The solstice is past and winter's on its way.'

Zen drowned his cigarette in the glass that Nieddu had previously used as an ashtray, then picked it up and carried it to the kitchen.

'Where did you take my drink?' Gilberto demanded.

'You don't need another drink,' Zen responded from the hideous kitchen. 'What you need is some food.'

'I'm not hungry.'

'That's why you need some food. "Hunger comes from eating, thirst is quenched by drinking." But not if you're drinking whatever this is.'

'White rum.'

Zen reappeared in the doorway.

'You need to eat, Gilberto.'

'There's nothing here to eat. Nothing you'd want to eat.'

'Then we'll go out.'

'I can't.'

'Why?'

Nieddu rolled up off the sofa and confronted Zen blearily.

'They all know me in this neighbourhood. And they know what's happened. The word's gone round. And if I show up, alone or with some male friend, the gossip and the sniggering is going to start. "Look, there's that Sardinian who cheated on his wife and got dumped." I can't take that, Aurelio. It used to be it was the women who suffered. "Her husband's run off with another woman." It was okay for the man, unless he was *cornuto*. But things have changed. I haven't been outside the building since it happened. I've been living on what was here, tinned stuff and pasta. I can't show my face in any of the restaurants round here.'

Zen smiled and took his arm.

'Fine, we'll go somewhere near my place. There are several

good places – nothing fancy, good solid home cooking – and no one will know you from Adam. Come on!'

The cab Zen called, from the cooperative he always used, arrived almost too soon. He still had not decided where to go. In the end he asked for Piazza del Risorgimento. They could walk from there.

'She lost her looks,' said Nieddu as the lighted streets slipped past.

'Rosa?'

A single, stiff nod was the only response.

'That happens,' Zen replied.

'Yes, but it happens in different ways to different women. That's what's so cruel. If it was uniform, like . . .'

He paused.

'Yes?' queried Zen.

'I don't know,' said Nieddu. 'Like something. There must be something it's like, right?'

'Probably.'

This is going to be a long night, thought Zen. But he already felt better, just being outside that apartment with its air of acquiescent despair.

'One minute she looked thirty, the next she looked sixty,' Nieddu went on. 'No, that's not quite right. There were a few years when she looked thirty most of the time, except in certain positions in a certain light when she suddenly looked sixty. After that, the balance tilted the other way. She looked sixty most of the time, except once in a while when she suddenly looked thirty again. That was the worst moment. Now she just looks sixty all the time.'

They had reached the embankment along the Tiber. Nieddu turned his eyes from the bright lights to the left and gazed out at the dark ditch on the other side.

'She had wonderful skin. Did you ever notice her skin, Aurelio? It was like a girl's, even when she was forty. And then it wasn't any more. It went all spongy and slack. It must have been dreadful for her, like wearing the finest silk all your life and then having to dress in cheap cotton. But it was tough on me, too. And so I stopped trying. With my affairs, I mean. It wasn't a conscious decision. I just didn't feel as guilty as I had before, so I didn't make as much effort.'

He emitted a harsh laugh.

'I've even thought that maybe that's what really pissed her off when she found out about me and Stefania. It wasn't just that I was fucking the help, it was that I couldn't even be bothered to cover it up properly. I'd got sloppy and unprofessional. That may have seemed like the last straw, the ultimate gesture of disrespect.'

The taxi dropped them in Piazza del Risorgimento. This dingy clearing in the urban jungle, with its eclectic mixture of imposing *umbertino* facades, the manically raucous traffic through which quaintly retro trams made their stately way, the central island laid out with tall pines and shrubbery that had seen better days, the inevitable grandiose and birdshit-bespattered statue, and the imposing line of walls surrounding the Vatican City State, had always appealed to Zen for some reason he would have found difficult to explain, still less justify.

Steering Nieddu firmly away from various bars he seemed inclined to enter, Zen led him to a trattoria on a street just off Via Ottaviano. He himself went there seldom, precisely because he kept it as a resource for those times when he didn't want to be instantly recognized by the owner and subjected to the barrage of chat, gossip and nosy questions which were the inevitable lot of any regular. Zen ordered a bowl of vegetable soup and half a roast chicken with green salad. Giorgio said he'd have the same and a litre of red wine.

'Anyway, what about you, Aurelio?' he asked in painfully *pro forma* tone of voice. 'I heard the Mafia tried to kill you.'

'That was a long time ago.'

'So where have you been all this time?'

'In Iceland, just recently.'

The wine arrived. Gilberto poured himself a large glass and downed it in one go.

'Iceland, eh? What's it like? Icy, I suppose.'

'No, that's Greenland.'

'Logical.'

After that, the conversation rather flagged. Gilberto, in the throes of alcoholic anorexia, picked at his food with the tentative air of a stranger in a strange land who has been invited to dine on unrecognizable local delicacies of whose nature and origin he is deeply suspicious. Zen ate his with a pleasure heightened by the fact that the soup had seen better days, the olive oil was of the industrial variety, the grated parmesan dried out, the chicken overcooked and too salty, and the salad leaves of the indestructible variety that resembled the rubber helmets that ladies at the Lido had used to wear during his childhood. It all reminded him very pleasantly of Maria Grazia's well-meaning culinary attempts, associated in his mind with the dull, cosy, slightly stifling family household from which he had spent a lifetime trying to escape, and which had now vanished, leaving only the empty shell for him to return to a little later in the evening.

'Do you want my advice, Gilberto?' he asked, pushing his plate away and lighting a cigarette.

'Not particularly. What do you know about it? You've never even been married.'

'Yes I have! Damn it, you were my best man.'

Nieddu made a gesture as if swatting at a fly he couldn't be bothered to kill.

'Oh, Luisella. That doesn't count.'

'Oh no?' Zen felt suddenly angry. 'And why not, might I ask? Because she didn't have perfect skin like your immortal beloved Rosa? Or because I wasn't unfaithful to her for years on end with every woman who came within reach?'

Nieddu shook his head calmly.

'No, it's because you didn't have kids.'

'It isn't a real marriage if you don't have children? That's absurd!'

'No, it's not. But you wouldn't know about that. Or about anything else concerning my situation. So you can keep your fucking advice to yourself, thank you very much.'

By now, Zen felt furious. He stood up, grabbed his coat, paid for his half of the meal and walked out. He had reached the corner of the main street when he heard a voice calling his name, and turned to see Gilberto Nieddu rushing after him, with one of the waiters from the restaurant in close pursuit.

'Aurelio! Stop!'

Zen stopped.

'Don't you dare talk like that to me, Gilberto,' he said frigidly. 'I don't give a damn about you or your problems. It serves you right.'

He turned away, only to be pulled back by Nieddu.

'No, no! It's not about that! I haven't got any money to pay for dinner. Can you lend me some?'

By now the waiter had caught them up, and was staring from one to the other with an anxious expression. Zen suddenly burst into laughter. He gave the waiter the same amount as he had already paid inside, plus a small tip for his exertions. When that transaction had been taken care of, he turned to his friend again, all anger now gone.

'Go, Gilberto,' he said. 'Go to Sassari. Go to the house. Don't phone, don't write, don't tell her you're coming. Just go.'

Nieddu looked suddenly shifty.

'Well, I don't know about that. Maybe later, if she's lucky. Once she starts to see reason. Let a little time pass, eh? Let her suffer a bit, realize what she's lost. Then I might go.'

'By then Rosa will have become accustomed to the situation, maybe even started to persuade herself that she enjoys it. And in a month the children will have started at a new school and will have a new circle of friends. Go now. Go tonight, if there's a flight. And if there isn't, hire a plane. You've got the money. Take a cab to the house and tell her that you've got a jet waiting at the airport to take the family home again.'

'It wouldn't be a jet. More likely a turboprop.'

'It doesn't matter what kind of aircraft it is, Gilberto!'

'But what about the brother?'

Zen looked at him solemnly.

'You really are a loser, aren't you?' he said.

'I make five times what you do, Zen, and pay a quarter as much tax!' Nieddu retorted violently.

'So what? If you don't get over to Sardinia right now and

bring back your wife and the mother of your children, then as far as I'm concerned you're a loser.'

He handed Nieddu a couple of thousand-lire coins.

'This'll get you home on the *metropolitana*. Call me when you have good news.'

When Aurelio Zen reached the address he still thought of as home, he had a very strange feeling: it was as if he were entering it for the first time. The spacious gloom of the entrance hall, the antique elevator in its wrought-iron cage, the neighbour's caged bird which mimicked the squeaky hinges of the front door to Zen's apartment; all these details, for years so worn with use as to have become transparent, now asserted themselves as fresh perceptions, potentially significant information about a territory never encountered before.

The lights still didn't work. By touch and instinct, aided at moments by the flame from his cigarette lighter, he found his way to the kitchen and then the cupboard where they had always kept a stock of candles for use during the power cuts which had at one time been a frequent occurrence. He bundled six of them together, tied them up with a length of twine chosen from the many odd pieces that Maria Grazia stored in a drawer because 'You never know when it might come in handy', then lit the wicks and made his way back to the living room, where he placed the bunch of candles on the table. The flames spluttered and wavered and then grew tall and steady, making the walls and ceiling glow in a way that reminded Zen irresistibly of the *camera ardente* at the funeral home where he had gone to view his mother's body.

'They don't put the body in the box,' said a voice in his head, 'they wrap the box around the body.'

No, that wasn't right. He'd been misled by the previous association with his mother's funeral. The word had been bottles, not body. 'They don't put the bottles in the box, they wrap the box around the bottles.' In some hospital, during one of the few lucid memories he had of that whole period. A young doctor was preparing to give him an injection of liquid drawn from one of a set of glass phials packed into a cardboard box on the trolley beside him. Zen had remarked, in an attempt at humour, that it must be hard work fitting all those tiny bottles into such a tight space. And the doctor had explained, adding that his brother worked in packaging and never tired of telling him that wraparound was the wave of the future.

But why had that voice come back to him now? He had often noticed that if he found himself humming some tune, there was usually a connection between the words, or title, or general context and associations of the music, and something that had been preoccupying him without his conscious awareness of it. The same must be the case here, he thought, but what possible connection could there be? Bottles, boxes, packaging, wraparound . . . None of these had any evident relevance. Nor did threats to his life and the resulting injuries, not to mention doctors or hospitals. He was finished with all that.

He moved his luggage into the bedroom where he used to sleep. Maria Grazia had stripped the bed before leaving. He didn't feel up to remaking it, so he fetched a pillow and some blankets from the linen cupboard in the hall, blew out the candles in the living room and groped his way back to the bedroom. The air was filled with the unctuous smoke of the candles, which made him realize that there had been a previous and not dissimilar odour in the apartment which he only now identified as the sweet-and-sour fetor of his mother's dying flesh. The thought made him close and lock the bedroom door behind him. A few minutes later he was lying fully clothed on his bed, wrapped up in his coat and the blankets. A few minutes after that he was asleep.

He awoke a moment later, or so it seemed. It was an instant and complete awakening with no memory of dreams, no drowsiness, and no evident cause. The room was silent and dark, apart from a faint glimmer coming up through the shutters from the street below. He lay on his back, staring up at the lamp hanging like a predatory bat from the ceiling. He had always loathed that lamp, he realized. Then he thought: Now that mamma's dead, I can get rid of it.

A sound broke the silence. It was difficult to say what might have caused it, but the source seemed clear. He lay quite still, listening intently. Eventually there was another sound, equally generic and almost inaudible, but it too had been located just outside the room, behind the locked door leading to the rest of the apartment. But that was absurd. Clearly there was no one out there. How could there be?

The silence then remained unbroken for so long that he almost convinced himself that he had imagined the earlier noises. Then he heard a distinct metallic scraping that he recognized instantly. Someone was turning the handle to his bedroom door.

'Who's there?' he shouted, sitting up in bed.

There was silence again, then a rapid series of ratchety clicks. Zen climbed out of bed as the door resounded under a tremendous blow.

'Who's that?' he yelled again.

Another blow, then another. The door was of seasoned oak, at least a hundred years old. It wouldn't give, unless the intruder had an axe, but sooner or later the catch must.

Zen groped in his coat pocket and found the device he had been given at the Ministry the previous afternoon. He clicked the button at the side to turn it on, then slid up the shield over the glowing red button and pressed it as another earthquake-like tremor hit the door.

What happened then was the last thing he had expected: the sound of a phone ringing in the room next door. It was only a moment later that he remembered that the phone had been cut off. There was a brief whisper of speech, followed by a number of unidentifiable sounds, then silence.

It was broken a few moments later by a distant siren that veered ever nearer and louder until it wound down from a strident shriek to a mild burble outside the building. Blue flashing lights added an intermittent brightness to the glimmer in the room, while a furious pounding and ringing sounded out in the stairwell and from the street. After a while it ceased, to be replaced by the sound of clattering boots on the stone steps and then in the room outside.

'Polizia!'

Zen felt a wave of overwhelming relief that made him realize just how scared he had been. He had heard that voice countless times before, and knew it well. It was the voice of a raw young patrol officer, himself scared even more, and knowing that his only hope of saving his reputation and possibly his life was to sound overwhelmingly masterful.

Zen unlocked and opened the door, and was immediately pinned in the glaring beams from two flashlights aimed right at his face.

'Good evening,' he said, holding up his empty hands. 'I am Dottor Zen.'

The two policemen in the room lowered their torches, creating a more even light.

'What's going on?' barked one.

'We received an all-points emergency call to assist you,' said a slightly steadier voice.

'Someone broke into my apartment.'

'The door was open when we got here,' replied the steadier voice immediately.

'Probably a burglar,' said the first patrolman.

'There have been a number of attempts on my life recently,' Zen replied in a studiously casual tone, as though this sort of thing was all in a day's work for him.

'The lights don't work,' said the steadier voice. 'Maybe they cut the wiring.'

'No, the fuse blew and I haven't had time to mend it. Now could you just check that whoever it was isn't still here, and perhaps try and find out how he got in?'

One of the two torches started searching the apartment. The other headed out to the stairway.

'No one,' reported the first voice, returning to the room.

He and Zen gazed at each other in the gloom hacked apart by his torch beam.

There was a rush of boots on the steps and his partner reappeared.

'The skylight at the very top of the stairs is wide open,' he announced. 'He must have been an agile little monkey, though. That window's a good three metres off the ground.'

'Well, thank you for your prompt response,' Zen said conclusively. 'Evidently on this occasion the whole thing was a false alarm. If you'll just inform headquarters about that, I won't keep you from your regular duties any longer.'

He saw them to the front door of the apartment, then bent down and examined the door itself. There was no sign that any force had been used to open it. It was only when he straightened up again that he noticed Giuseppe, the janitor of the building. He was clad in pyjamas and a worn plaid dressing gown, and was lurking on the flight of stairs leading up to the landing.

'Is everything all right, *dottò*?' he asked.

Zen took out the key to his apartment.

'You didn't give this to anyone while I was away, did you?'

Giuseppe's face assumed an expression of righteous indignation.

'Absolutely not! It was locked up in the safe the whole time along with the duplicate sets.'

Zen nodded.

'Very well. I just wondered.'

'If you'd told me you were coming back, I'd have arranged for the electricity and gas to be on,' Giuseppe added. 'I'll do it tomorrow, first thing.'

'Don't bother. I shan't be living here any more.'

Giuseppe took a few moments to digest this statement. So did Zen himself.

'You're moving?' Giuseppe queried.

'I'm leaving. A new work assignment. I shan't be based in Rome any longer. I'll contact the owners and tell them to cancel the lease as soon as possible. They should be able to find a new tenant quite quickly. Unless you have someone in mind, of course.'

Giuseppe nodded in a dazed way. Clearly this, coming on top of the break-in and the appearance of the policemen, was just too much to deal with at this hour of the morning. He started to turn away, then paused.

'Maybe that colleague of yours would like it.'

'Which colleague?'

'I don't recall the name. It was a long time ago, right after that terrible bomb business. He came by to pick up some papers from work you'd left in the apartment. When he handed me back the key, he said what a nice place it was.'

'You gave him the key?'

'Of course. He showed me his identification card. It was just like yours, *dottò*. Well, different photo and name, of course, but the real thing. And he said he worked with you, so I let him in. I mean, I knew you were in hospital, so you couldn't come yourself. That was all right, wasn't it?'

'Yes. Yes, of course. Good night, Giuseppe.'

'Good night, *dottò*.'

Zen went back inside, closing but not locking the door. What was the point?

'Don't look them in the eye, and never turn your back.'

This time the voice was in the air, not in his head. He could feel its vibrations, although he knew there was no one there. Then another voice, this one internal, added, 'They don't put the bottles in the box, they wrap the box around the bottles.'

He lit the knotted candles on the table and stood there in the gradually waxing light, staring at the chair in which his mother had always sat to watch banal television programmes which her addled mind had transmuted into richer, stranger material. Something was trying to tell him something, but what was it?

For the first time, it occurred to him to look at his watch. It was a little after three in the morning. After a momentary hesitation, he went back into his bedroom and found the shelf on which he kept his Pozzorario railway timetable, the front cover festooned with anachronistic advertisements for various hotels *con tutti i conforti a prezzi modici*. Not for the first time, he wondered if anyone ever selected a hotel on the basis of these rather desperate-sounding appeals, and if so who. The timetable itself was a year out of date, but Zen knew that the schedules of the night trains were virtually invariable. After a few minutes' search, he found an express from Reggio di Calabria to Milan that stopped at the station of Roma Tiburtina just after four o'clock. He repacked his bags, then called for a taxi. The dispatcher said that Taranto 64 would be there in about ten minutes.

Zen spent the interval wandering about the apartment, apart from his mother's room, which he did not enter, and wondering if there was anything he wanted to keep. Nothing, he concluded, with a surprising shiver of pleasure. He'd hire a company to haul everything away and dispose of it for whatever price they could get. He wasn't even going to think about it. It could all go.

A car drew up outside. Zen took a last look around the disturbingly notional space which had been his home for so many years and then, failing once again to be moved, picked up his bags, closed and locked the door and walked downstairs.

Fortunately the driver of Taranto 64 proved to be one of the few night cabbies in Rome who didn't want to share his life story, political views, family problems and forecast for next season's football championship with his fare. He just shut up and drove. There was almost no traffic, and they arrived at their destination in fifteen minutes. Zen over-tipped the soothingly reticent driver, walked inside the station and bought a first-class single ticket to Florence.

The platforms were deserted. By day, Tiburtina was a busy suburban station serving commuters and shoppers, but at this hour of the night it functioned purely as a stopping place to switch crews on long-haul trains without going into the terminus and having to change locomotives as well. Zen wandered into the bar and bought a cappuccino which he nursed until the clangour of a bell and then an incomprehensible announcement over the loudspeaker system warned of the imminent arrival of his train.

It consisted mainly of sleeping cars, and most of the seating carriages were empty. Zen could easily have had a first-class compartment to himself, but for various reasons he chose instead to share one with two other men. One was almost caricaturally Sicilian, the other less easy to place. Both had evidently been dozing, and went back to stertorous sleep as soon as the train started again. After a while, Zen joined them.

When he woke, they were in the Arno valley and dawn was just starting to break. No details were yet visible outside, but the rugged mass of the Apennines to the east showed black against the gradually lightening sky. It felt good to be out of Rome. He would never live there again if he could help it, he realized.

He disembarked in Florence at the transit station of Rifredi, and grabbed an espresso before the arrival of an early local train to the terminus at Santa Maria Novella. In the piazza outside, the blue buses that served the region were starting to gather. One of the drivers told him that there was a service to Versilia leaving at eight o'clock. That left about an hour to kill. He went across the street to the Lazzi office, bought a ticket and left his luggage behind the counter, then set off towards the Mercato Centrale.

Zen had used this huge covered public market – the largest in Europe, as the locals characteristically claimed – as an early-morning breakfast venue before, in the course of brief trips to or through the city on assignments he could no longer remember. It was a short and pleasant walk from the station through the twisty, narrow, empty streets, and like all markets it came to bustling life at an hour when the rest of the city was still brushing its teeth.

When Zen arrived, the stallholders were still putting the finishing touches to their displays of produce and their clients had not yet materialized, but the food stands were doing a brisk trade from the market workers who clustered around each one, squabbling good-naturedly among themselves, joking, gossiping, miming excessive emotions of every kind, and from time to time breaking off to nag the unflappable serving staff into getting a move on with their order. No dainty pastries and lukewarm milky coffee for these men. They had a hard morning's work ahead, lugging around sides of meat and whole hams and cheeses, and were tucking into crusty rolls stuffed with boiled tripe or beef, washed down with tumblers of Chianti sloshed from plastic-wrapped flasks.

Zen fought his way to the front just as another lump of beef emerged from the steaming cauldron set over a gas ring. He pointed to it, then to the wine, handed over some money and edged back out of the throng to let someone else have a turn. Eventually he found a spot at an angle of the market building where he could park his glass of wine on the railing, and proceeded to munch away. Reaching into his coat pocket for the bunch of tissues he had grabbed from the dispenser to wipe off his greasy lips, he felt a more substantial paper product.

Extracting it, he read 'Þórunn Sigurðardóttir', and felt so happy not to be in Iceland that he went straight back to the stand and ordered another roll and another glass of wine.

How ridiculous it all was! Everything that had happened to him in the last few weeks seemed like a dream which makes perfect sense until you wake up and realize just how gullible you've been. That business on the coast and in the plane, the voices in his head and all the rest of it . . . It all amounted to nothing more than a flurry of coincidental nonsense, swirls of mental mud thrown up by the physical and mental ordeal that he had been through. But now it was over.

He finished his second roll and the rest of the wine and checked his watch. Just ten minutes left to catch the bus back to the coast. Perfect. He wondered if Gemma would still be at the beach. Or had he dreamed her too? In a few hours he would find out.

Outside the covered market, the street traders were now setting up their stalls laden with clothing, leather goods, CDs, tapes and videos. Zen walked through them, thinking only of catching his bus, until his eye was caught by some items of clothing. They were T-shirts, hanging from a wire suspended at the end of one of the carts. The colours differed, but the words printed on them were all the same: 'Life's a beach'.

He stopped and fingered one of the garments. Noticing Zen's interest, the vendor came over and named a variety of prices in rapidly declining order. Zen shook his head, but the man unhooked one of the shirts and turned it over to display the alleged quality of the cloth and manufacture. On the back of the shirt, in exactly the same lettering, was printed 'And then you die'.

Zen waved the salesman aside and hurried on his way, turning the foreign phrase over in his mind. *La vita è una spiaggia e poi si muore.* It made no sense. Perhaps it was some idiomatic expression he didn't understand. There were so many things about English speakers he didn't understand, like Ellen, his one-time American girlfriend asking him, 'Why are all the things I like either fattening or bad for me?' He'd shrugged and replied, 'Because you like the wrong things.'

It had seemed self-evident to him, hardly worth saying, but Ellen had reacted as though he'd slapped her. 'I can't help what I like!' she'd wailed. He'd sensed then that Americans liked to like things that were bad for them. It added a frisson of sin to their indulgence, and a self-righteous glow to abstinence.

'Life's a beach and then you die.' Absurd. Another piece of dream jetsam with no significance. People would buy clothes with any nonsense on them as long as it was in English. For all they knew, they could be walking round sporting a shirt or jacket which said 'I'm a Complete Idiot.' It didn't matter. English was chic.

He emerged into the piazza in front of Santa Maria Novella, retrieved his baggage from the Lazzi office and climbed aboard the bus just as the driver started the engine in a cloud of diesel fumes.

LUCCA

The warm evening light washed down, its heat glowing back up off the worn flagstones where four boys were playing football. Couples and clusters of locals stood about gossiping in a drowsy harmony punctuated by the brief appearance of bicyclists transiting in a leisurely manner from one portal of the small oval piazza to another. In the midst of it all, at an outlying table of a café, protected from the sun's rays by a blue *ombrellone*, Aurelio Zen sat clad in a new cream linen suit and his Panama hat, lingering over the dregs of a coffee and smiling inanely at the sheer blissful pleasure of it all.

For the first time in his life, he felt himself to be a complete gentleman of leisure. He had spent the intervening ten days at the beach, sunning himself, relaxing, and lunching or dining with Gemma either at a variety of local restaurants – including one in a village perched on a crag at the end of a hair-raising mountain road up which she had driven without complaint or comment – or at the villa where he had reinstalled himself. Nothing had 'happened' between them, but there seemed every reason to suppose that something was about to, and it was their very sense of the inevitability of this that had precluded any hasty moves on either side. Nevertheless, the day before, Gemma had definitely made a move of some kind by inviting Zen to dinner.

'I should invite you,' he had replied.

'You can't.'

'Why not?'

'Because the invitation is to my house.'

At these words, the ancient core of Zen's cerebrum, the only part he had ever really trusted, told him that something significant was going to happen this evening. Hence the new – and, truth be told, ruinously expensive – linen suit, hence the tingle of pleasurable anticipation transforming the mundane scenes in the piazza of this sleepy provincial town into signs and symbols of powers still in effect from when the place had been a Roman amphitheatre. Unspeakable things must have happened in the space where those *ragazzi* were kicking their ball around, seemingly recklessly and with complete abandon, yet always ensuring that it did not cause any bother or inconvenience to any of the other players in the arena. That was part of the game, one of the rules.

Something was going to happen, of that he was sure, but he had no clear idea what, still less any sense that he could control the event in any decisive way. On his reappearance at the beach, Gemma had initially seemed a bit cool and distant. Zen had explained his abrupt absence as being due to 'business', to which she had responded by a curt nod, as if to say 'If you have your secrets, so have I.'

Nevertheless, he could not help grudgingly admitting to himself that the prognostications were good. He hadn't heard a word from the Ministry over his misuse of the high-tech communication device they had given him, sending out an all-points urgent alarm over some burglar breaking into his apartment in Rome. He had, however, heard from Gilberto Nieddu, who had taken Zen's advice, made the necessary penitential pilgrimage to Sardinia, and convinced Rosa to return home with him and the children. Her terms, according to Gilberto, had been surprisingly mild: 'Very well, but next time – if there is a next time – I won't just leave you, I'll leave you for dead.' Zen had enthusiastically seconded Nieddu's opinion that coming from Rosa this amounted to a declaration of total forgiveness and eternal love.

Zen had also visited the hospital at Pietrasanta once again, this time to have the stitches on his knuckles removed. The doctors had taken the opportunity to examine his general progress one last time, and had pronounced him surprisingly well advanced on the way to total recovery. Better still, the last traces of the *huldufolk* had vanished along with the stitches. He had heard no more voices, had enjoyed dreamless sleep, and in general seemed fully integrated back into the common lot of humanity.

This of course included a general uncertainty, and a measure of anxiety, about the future. The fact of the matter was that he liked Gemma, to the extent that he had got to know her, and that he desired her as a woman. He had some reason to suppose that she felt something similar where he was concerned, but that was all. He knew nothing about her in any depth, and almost everything she knew about him was either lies or a distortion of the truth. The most probable scenario therefore seemed to be that they would either end up in bed this evening, or some evening soon, or they wouldn't, but in either case that would be as far as it went. Both of them came with lengthy and elaborate histories, and neither had shown much interest in investigating or explaining them, much to Zen's relief. This made for a trouble-free *divertimento* in the short run, but suggested that the longer-term prospects were tenuous in the extreme. There was just not enough to hold them together, to give them a reason for not going their separate ways. Even with a marriage and children, not to mention decades of intimacy at an age when the personality is still malleable, Gilberto and Rosa had come within a breath of parting for ever. What lasting hope could there be for two strangers at mid-life, with nothing more in common than that they happened to be seated in opposite *ombrelloni* at Franco's bathing establishment, and seemed to get along and be mildly attracted to one another?

He glanced at his watch and stood up with a sardonic grin at his own fatuousness in taking all this so seriously. A brand-new suit, a bad case of stage fright, and, yes, some roses would be a good idea, just to complete the caricature. One little bomb under the car he'd been travelling in and a couple of half-hearted attempts by some Mafia thug to silence him, and here he was convinced that a casual and probably purely conventional dinner invitation – Gemma's way of paying him back for his hospitality to her – was the hour of destiny. But it would still be interesting to see her apartment. One could learn a lot from the things people had chosen to surround themselves with, especially if the choice had been made with a view to preventing you doing so.

A lengthy and lazily uncoordinated peal of bells from various churches and towers began to ring out seven o'clock as he walked the length of the piazza and out into the street beyond, which bent and narrowed at the point where it would have passed through the original Roman walls. The cramped space between the tall medieval buildings to either side was packed with tall, elegant Lucchesi on foot or on bikes who wove their way through the seemingly impenetrable mass of pedestrians with the same *disinvoltura* that the future soccer stars had displayed in the piazza.

A news-stand he passed was displaying copies of a satirical review whose headline read, 'Medical Breakthrough Reveals Why Pisans Are Born – No Cure In Sight.' Zen smiled indulgently and moved on. Unlike most other countries, at least Italy did not use neighbouring nations as its stereotypes for crass stupidity. The universal butt of such low humour was the *carabinieri*, but every region had its own ritually despised city, whose inhabitants were depicted as cretinous scum who would believe anything and achieve nothing. In his native Veneto, the traditional target was Vicenza; here in Tuscany it was evidently Pisa, and such gags would have a particular appeal here in industrious, mercantile Lucca, so near to yet so far from the neighbouring *città di mare*, with its untrustworthy crew of brigands and adventurers with a weather eye always out for one-off deals and a quick killing.

He found a flower shop and ordered a dozen red roses, then wondered if this might look a bit pointed. After a long discussion of the intricacies of the situation with the florist, who had the soft voice and perfect tact of all the townsfolk Zen had encountered, he emerged with a bouquet of yellow roses and turned left off the main street towards the address which Gemma had given him. I like this place, he thought as he strode along. I could be happy here. Despite being entirely landlocked, Lucca reminded him in some indefinable way of Venice. It was a question of its scale, its look and feel of placid security, and above all the politely reticent manners of its citizens, refined by centuries of trade and commerce.

The moment he turned into Via del Fosso, he felt even more at home. The name – Ditch Street – was not attractive, but the thing itself was: a broad avenue of fine buildings to either side of a stone-embanked canal. The trickle of channelled water here was evidently fresh rather than tidal, the buildings more recent and everything on a smaller scale, but the concept was as familiar to Zen as his own face. This was a miniature version of the neighbourhood in Venice where he had grown up. The district must originally have been outside the Roman and medieval city, open fields later enfolded within the imposing line of redbrick baroque walls visible ahead of him. This is where the middle-class merchants of that time would have built their spacious and imposing mansions, leaving the clogged *centro* and its anachronistic palaces and slums to the decaying nobles and penniless plebs.

He found the house and mounted the step. Gemma had warned him that there were no names beside the buttons of the entry phone, but that hers was the second from the bottom. Almost as soon as Zen rang, the buzzer sounded and the front door unlatched. For a moment he was disconcerted by the lack of any preliminary query, but then realized that there had been no need of that. Gemma was expecting him and him alone.

As if to confirm this impression, the door to her apartment was slightly ajar. Zen knocked lightly and then entered, the bunch of roses concealed behind his back.

'Gemma?'

There was no one in the hallway. She was probably in the kitchen, putting the finishing touches to their meal. Zen smiled, touched by this discreet message. He was being received as an old friend, a member of the family almost, one of the privileged few for whom *complimenti* would have been an insulting mark of coldness and distance. He walked down the hall and into the living room.

'Gemma?'

But the person in the room was not Gemma. To the left of the door, just out of immediate eyeshot, stood a youngish man with blond hair and a thin moustache, wearing faded jeans and an open-necked shirt in a brilliant shade of orange.

'*Buona sera, dottore,*' he said.

My God, thought Zen, it's what's-his-name, Gemma's jealous husband. He'd imagined him like this – young, lithe, athletic – but then reminded himself that whenever he read or heard about someone called by the same name as his boyhood friend in Venice, he always imagined them like that. For him, anyone called Tommaso would be always be gifted with eternal youth. In this case, however, he had been right.

'Gemma's in the dining room,' the man went on. 'Over there to your right. No, please, after you.'

Feeling utterly ridiculous with his pathetic bouquet of roses, Zen obediently walked over to the doorway, the man following. Had Gemma told her husband that he was coming? Was this some sort of weird humiliation she had decided to inflict on him in return for his unexplained disappearance from the beach?

The moment he crossed the threshold to the next room, these thoughts vanished. Gemma was there all right. She was sitting in one of the dining chairs right opposite Zen, turned away from a small table elaborately laid for two. Twists of synthetic orange cord secured her arms and chest to the chair. Her mouth was covered by a wide strip of metallic silver tape and her eyes were wild.

Zen instinctively started towards her, only to be halted by a voice.

'Don't touch, please. You know the old saying. "Pretty to look at, delightful to hold, but if it gets broken consider it sold."'

Zen swung round, letting the bouquet fall to the floor in front of Gemma. There was a different man behind him now, totally bald and clean-shaven. In one hand he held a blond wig and the wispy moustache, in the other an automatic pistol fitted with a silencer.

'Against the wall please, *dottore,*' he said, pointing with the gun. 'You are familiar with the position, I take it.'

Zen splayed himself out against the wall, hands and feet

widely spaced. He felt the pressure of the gun barrel in his back.

'Don't stain my suit,' he stupidly said.

The man laughed.

'Don't worry. By the time I've finished with you, your suit will be the last thing on your mind.'

Hands frisked him quickly and professionally. That professionalism, and the sound of the laugh, finally made everything clear. The man's next words, as he found and removed the communication device that Zen had been given at the Ministry, merely served as confirmation.

'Ah, yes, your little squawkbox. Just as well I still have a few friends in the business. All right, turn around.'

The man tossed Zen's belongings down on the floor beside the wig and moustache he had been wearing.

'Still don't recognize me?' he asked teasingly.

Zen did, but the memory brought only despair. He said nothing.

'Really? Does the name Alfredo Ferraro mean anything to you?'

Zen creased his brow and then shook his head.

'I'm afraid not.'

'You're afraid not. Well, *dottore*, you're right to be afraid. But it's a shame you don't remember Alfredo. Some of us do. Some of us remember him very well, as well as what happened to him and who was responsible. Which of course is why I'm here.'

He held out the hand holding the pistol in a mock salutation.

'Roberto Lessi.'

Zen forced his brow to furrow again.

'Lessi? Wait, I do remember someone by that name. Yes, that's right. He was an officer with the *carabinieri*'s ROS division. He saved my life when I was on that assignment in Sicily.'

The man laughed his flat, hard laugh again.

'Very good, Dottor Zen, very good.'

'You're Lessi?' gasped Zen, as though the thought had only just struck him. 'You look different, somehow. Or maybe that Mafia bomb affected my memory. Anyway, I only saw you that once, and at night.'

Lessi stared at him with eyes that told Zen how close he was to death. He looked about him distractedly, taking in every detail of the situation.

'No, actually you saw me four times, if we're only counting last year.'

The man's leisurely tone gave Zen a flicker of hope for the first time. If Lessi wanted to talk, to explain and to justify himself, then there might conceivably be time to do what was necessary.

'That time out in the country near Etna was the last,' the gunman went on. 'Before that, there was the time we picked you up in the street outside your apartment, the time on the ferry to Malta, and then earlier that evening, when you gunned down my partner Alfredo Ferraro in cold blood.'

'What do you mean, cold blood?' Zen demanded instinctively. 'He had just strangled one man and was about to shoot me.'

Lessi smiled.

'Ah, so you do remember Alfredo after all. I rather thought you did, to be honest. Perhaps you remember the truth about that bomb, too. You must do.'

Zen glanced at the statically frantic figure of Gemma, just to check that her position was exactly as he had recalled it.

'Of course I do,' he said. 'The Mafia tried to murder me on the way back from my meeting with Don Gaspare Limina. He promised me safe conduct, but that was a lie. They just wanted time to get clear and to do the job far away from anywhere connected with them.'

Roberto Lessi shook his head in mock disappointment.

'Sorry, dottore. You're very convincing and I almost believe you, but in the end it's too much of a stretch. Your brain worked very well indeed when we met in Sicily and on the ferry to Malta, and I think it's working just fine now.'

He was right, but that wasn't the point. The point was to start the ballet. Zen took a couple of apparently casual steps to his left.

'Of course it is!' he protested vehemently. 'That's what happened. So what the hell are you doing breaking in here and threatening me and Signora Santini? You realize that this means the end of your career.'

Lessi had also moved slightly to the left, instinctively compensating to keep the same distance and angle between himself and his adversary.

'My career has already ended, *dottore*. We screwed up, you see. Well, my ex-colleagues did.'

'What are you talking about?' Zen snapped irritably, fidgeting another step around the invisible circle.

'You remember when the Corleone clan killed Judge Falcone and his wife?' Lessi replied. 'They almost screwed up too. They planted a ton of explosives in that culvert under the motorway into Palermo from the airport, then blew the charge a second or two too early, for fear that Falcone's car would pass by before it detonated. They knew they only had one chance, and so they panicked. In the end Falcone was killed anyway, but only because he had insisted on driving when he was met at the airport. So he and his wife were sitting in the front seats of their car and took the full force of the blast, even though they were still some distance from the culvert. The *carabinieri* in the lead escort car, including some of my closest friends, were all wiped out. As for the chauffeur, he was seated in the back, where Falcone and his wife would have been if the judge hadn't had his little whim. So they were killed and he survived.'

Lessi had stopped moving, intent on his story, but Zen kept going, restlessly tracing a figure of short steps one way and another, but always two to the left and one to the right.

'Well, *dottore*, the reason you're alive is just the reverse of that scenario. The men who set the bomb and were responsible for detonating it were stationed on the hillside above the bridge your car crossed. Just for the record, they had no idea that you were in it. They had been told that the passengers were some Mafia thugs who we were eliminating as a routine "dirty war" tactic designed to stir up trouble between the rival clans.'

Zen kept moving, glancing down at his feet as though they hurt him. Like the professional he was, even while fixated on his tale, Lessi responded by keeping pace in the same clockwise direction, keeping Zen always opposite him and safely beyond striking range, about two metres distant.

'When they found out the truth, they were horrified, or at least pretended to be,' he went on. 'I tried to pass it off as a mistake, but I was forced to resign anyway. That hurt, I can tell you. I'd been expecting a little more cooperation and understanding from men I'd been working with for all these years.'

He coughed out another laugh.

'Loyalty doesn't mean a damn thing in this country any more.'

Still continuing his ritualistic shuffle, Zen looked Lessi in the eye for the first time.

'But they blew the bomb.'

'They blew the bomb, just like our friends in the Mafia did with Falcone. Unfortunately in their case they blew it a couple of seconds too *late*. I watched the whole thing from the ridge on the other side of the river bed, counting down to give the signal by turning the motorbike's headlights on. But your driver seemed to speed up suddenly, and by the time I flashed and the others responded, the car had crossed the bridge. And since you were sitting in the front, it was that poor dumb cop who came along to hold your hand who was killed, while you and the driver got off with a few scrapes and bruises.'

'It was rather more serious than that.'

'Who cares? The only thing that matters is that you're still alive. Alfredo isn't. Plus you have enough evidence to send me away for life, if you could ever get anyone to believe you.'

'I couldn't. You know that.'

'No, I don't. I'd like to think so. I'd even go so far to admit that it's probable that no one would believe you. But it's not certain. And I want certainty at this point in my life, Zen. I've been eking out an existence of sorts with my relatives in Pisa, but sooner or later my savings are going to run out, and you know what I can expect then? At best some dead-end job as a private *guardia giurata* standing like a target outside a bank all day.'

Zen took two more steps to his left.

'Stay put!' Lessi yelled suddenly, raising his pistol.

Zen shrugged self-deprecatingly.

'It's my feet. Bunions. Runs in the family. If I have to stand still for any time, they start acting up.'

'Fine. Just don't try acting up yourself. Can you imagine how I've felt? Fired from my job, my partner killed, and meanwhile your career is all set to go into orbit just as soon as the injured hero of the Mafia wars decides that he's sufficiently rested to trudge back to the office and tell the press and some keen young investigating magistrate with a reputation to make that his memory has suddenly come back and the true story of what happened that night in Sicily is rather different from what everyone has been led to believe.'

Lessi gestured with the pistol.

'Up against the wall again,' he said. 'It'll be easier for both of us.'

Zen gestured frantically.

'But what about Signora Santini?' he said. 'She has nothing to do with any of this.'

'She does now. I've been monitoring your cellphone conversations, you see. Quite easily done, if you have access to the equipment. So I knew when you were expected this evening, and got here in plenty of time. Your girlfriend seemed quite surprised to see me, and naturally we got chatting once I'd tied her up. I needed to tell someone, you see, and I knew there wouldn't be time once you arrived. So I'm afraid it has to be both of you. It would anyway, if that's any consolation. I'm a pro, just like you, Zen. We don't leave jobs half done.'

That was it, then. Still over two metres to go, and the clock had apparently run out. Lessi had explained everything he had to say to Gemma earlier, and now had no further need to talk. Which left only one very risky possibility, totally dependent on Lessi being the 'pro' he claimed to be, in control of the situation, his trigger finger relaxed.

Zen shrugged helplessly and staggered to his left, in the direction Lessi had indicated. His shoe caught the base of a sideboard leaning against the wall, and he went tumbling down to the floor, a comic buffoon unable to make his way about the room without falling over.

Lessi laughed.

'Maybe I've been overestimating you,' he said. 'Come on, get up! On your feet and up against the wall.'

Zen clambered up again, then slumped on to his knees.

'I can't believe this is happening,' he whined.

'Well, it is.'

Zen lurched up once more, glancing about him as though totally in shock. He had now made up the circular distance. All that remained was the final and most dangerous move, and the question of whether Gemma had understood. But there was no point in worrying about that.

Turning, he took two long, slow steps towards Lessi, his hands outspread in a gesture of appeal.

'Look, can't we just . . .'

Lessi instantly stepped backwards, so as to maintain the distance between them. He was just starting to say something when Gemma kicked him viciously in the back of the knees. A shot went off, wide to the right, and then Zen sprang forward as Lessi crumpled, kicking him hard in the groin and following it up with a blow to the man's chin. He grabbed the hand holding the pistol, swung Lessi around and fell heavily on top of him.

For a moment Lessi lay limp on the floor, groaning. Zen raised his weight slightly off the man's body and went for the pistol. Instantly Lessi swirled up and around. In desperation, Zen grabbed a handful of the scattered roses and rasped the thorny stems across his opponent's face. Lessi screamed and instinctively brought up his hands to cover his eyes. Zen sank his teeth into the hand holding the gun, prised it loose by the barrel, and hit the other man again and again over the head with short, rapid blows, drawing blood from the scalp.

Lessi groaned and collapsed, murmuring something Zen didn't understand. When he was finally still, Zen transferred the butt of the pistol to his hand, crossed himself rapidly, stuck the barrel into the base of Lessi's skull and fired three times.

A long time seemed to pass. Finally Zen stood up, thinking

of the time he had put up some shelving at the family home in Venice, years ago. He felt the same calm, quiet satisfaction now, the same modest pride at a job well done. That house must be worth a fortune now, he thought.

He was brought out of this complacent mood of professional satisfaction by a savage kick to his calf which almost brought him down on top of his victim. He immediately bent over Gemma, tore the metallic tape off her mouth and then kissed her impulsively. Some of the adhesive backing remained on her lips, and even when the kiss was over it took a moment for them to unglue themselves.

'Hang on,' Zen told her, heading for the kitchen. He returned with a bread knife with which he cut through the cord binding Gemma to the chair. Then he helped her to her feet, rubbing the sore patches on her wrists anxiously.

'Let's just make sure the bastard's dead first,' said Gemma, pulling herself free.

She bent over Lessi's body while Zen stood back, the pistol in one hand and the knife in the other.

'There's no pulse,' Gemma commented, standing up again.

'Are you sure?'

'All registered pharmacists have to take first aid courses and refreshers. Believe me, he's dead.'

She sighed loudly and turned towards the living room.

'I'll call the police.'

'No!'

Zen's tone was so peremptory that she looked at him half in startlement and half in anger.

'What do you mean?'

'We mustn't do that.'

'Are you out of your mind? This man came here and tried to kill us. Instead you killed him and I've got a corpse on my floor. Of course I must call them. You're a policeman yourself, he told me. You of all people should realize that.'

'Did he tell you that he was a policeman too?' Zen asked.

Gemma looked irritatedly confused.

'No, but what's that got to do with it?'

'Everything.'

'And what's that supposed to mean?' she almost shouted.

Zen placed the knife on the sideboard, put the gun in his pocket and took her arm.

'The situation's a bit more complicated than you think. Or maybe it isn't. I'm still slightly in shock. Isn't adrenaline great stuff? Come into the next room and I'll explain. It won't take long. Then go ahead and call 113 if you want.'

Gemma shook him off.

'We can do this right here,' she said, confronting him. 'First, a few questions. Your name is Zen?'

'Yes.'

'What sort of name is that?

'Venetian.'

'And you're a policeman?'

'Yes.'

'So everything you've told me up to now was a lie.'

Zen shrugged.

'I don't know about everything. But I lied about quite a bit, yes.'

'Then why should I believe anything you say now?'

'Because now I don't need to lie. And I won't, Gemma. I won't ever tell you any more lies, whatever happens.'

She looked for a moment as though she wanted to believe him.

'But why now? Why not then?'

Zen hesitated for a moment. Then he recalled the phrase that one of his escorts had used when they drove him to Pisa airport after the shooting on the beach.

'I was not ordered to tell the truth. If you like, I'll explain why. But first we have to decide what to do about this.'

He gestured at Lessi's corpse.

'We call the police,' Gemma answered. 'We explain what happened. You shot him in self-defence after he'd threatened to kill us both. I'll testify to that. There won't be any problems.'

Zen shook his head.

'It's not as easy as that. Come and sit down and I'll try and explain. Afterwards, if you still want to call the police, I won't try to stop you.'

144

He started towards the living room.

'Not in there,' Gemma snapped. 'If you insist on boring me, come into the kitchen. We're a couple of murderers, for God's sake! There's no point in being formal.'

In the bright, modern kitchen she gulped down a large glass of water, then another. Then she produced a bottle of white wine from the fridge and poured a glass for each of them. For the first time, Zen noticed what she was wearing. The same bare legs, the same sandals, but for this evening at home a very simple sleeveless dress in some soft pale-green material, tied at the left side of her waist. She wore flat gold earrings, but her hair looked less studied this time, her nails were unpainted and her make-up minimal. She looked fabulous, he thought, as if that mattered.

'I'll try and make this brief,' he told her, 'because if you're going to call the cops, you'll have to do it in the next few minutes. But we're safe here for the moment. Lessi was almost certainly operating alone. An anonymous break-in and two dead bodies was his idea, hence the wig and moustache. Even if one of the neighbours had seen him enter, the description wouldn't have been recognized. He was counting on no one knowing what had really happened, and therefore he almost certainly didn't tell anyone else about it. He may have had friends who would help him out in minor ways, like giving him the odd tip as to my whereabouts, but he couldn't count on them backing him up when a double murder was involved.'

He paused, smiling ingratiatingly and hoping that Gemma believed all this.

'It's unlikely that anyone heard the shots, but if you decide to make this official then the time of death will be established more or less accurately. So we can't dither around too long. Here's all I have to say, and I'd just ask you to hear me out before making a decision. Lessi's dead, but he was a member of an elite unit with a very strong *esprit de corps*. He admitted himself that he still had . . .'

A voice sounded out in the courtyard outside. Gemma went over to the open window.

'*Ciao*, Antonella!' she called down.

The other woman said something Zen didn't catch.

'No, no, I was just opening a bottle of spumante,' Gemma replied. 'I have an old friend over to dinner.'

'*Bene, bene,*' the other voice replied. '*Allora buon appetito.*'

'*Altrettanto.*'

Gemma turned back to Zen.

'You were saying?'

'I said that Lessi must have still had "a few friends in the business", as he put it. They'll have friends too. Lessi may have been regarded as a rotten apple, but if they find out that I killed him all that will change. The ranks will close. Believe me, they'll get even, one way or another. They may not kill me, but the prospect will be something I'll be living with for the rest of my life. You too, if we're still together.'

Gemma looked at him in a startlingly new way which he couldn't interpret at all.

'But what's the alternative?'

Her voice had changed too. Zen shrugged wearily, suddenly aware how absurd it was to even be making this appeal.

'He'd have to disappear. If we're ever going to go back to leading normal lives, we'd have to dispose of the body in such a way that it would never be found, and would be completely unidentifiable if it were. That would, of course, make you an accessory. So you're right, come to think of it. Call the police. You'd be crazy not to.'

He turned away and took a swallow of wine.

'How could we do that?' asked Gemma.

Zen tightened his grip on the glass, but didn't turn round.

'Do what?'

'Hide the body in the way you mentioned.'

He laughed lightly, as though she had posed some theoretical philosophical problem of no real concern to either of them.

'Well, I don't know,' he said, turning to face her but not looking her in the eyes. 'I suppose there must be places up in the mountains where it might not be found for a while. Some abandoned mine or old railway tunnel. But I don't know of any, and I don't expect you do either.'

'What about at sea?'

He looked at her now, but laughed again.

146

'That would be perfect, of course, but how are we going to manage it? We can't very well take the corpse down to Livorno in the car and dump it over the rail of the Elba ferry.'

Gemma finished her wine and set her glass down with a distinct clink.

'Tommaso has a boat. Well, it belongs to both of us, theoretically.'

This time, Zen didn't laugh.

'We can hardly drag Tommaso into this.'

'We don't need to. The marina has a set of keys. They'll give them to me.'

Zen stared at her in total perplexity. Gemma opened the refrigerator.

'It's all right, you don't have to decide right away,' she said. 'Shall we have something to eat?'

Zen pointed to the dining room, where Roberto Lessi's head was just visible.

'But what about . . .?' he said.

Gemma looked at his vaguely pointing hand, then turned back to the fridge.

'Fuck him, he's dead,' she replied. 'I bought this fabulous red mullet specially for tonight, but I can't face cooking it now. Would some starters and a little pasta do? It's about all I'm up for, frankly.'

She set a dish of *antipasti di mare* and a loaf of bread on the small table near the window which must have served her and her husband as their breakfast nook, then turned up the heat under a cauldron of water on the stove. Zen noted that the pasta water had been started but then turned off.

'So he arrived about a quarter of an hour before I was due,' he said. 'Twenty minutes, more like. He had plenty of time to talk.'

'How do you know that?'

'I'm a detective. I'll explain later.'

'Very well. Shall we eat?'

Zen just stood there staring.

'What is it?' demanded Gemma, sitting down.

'Nothing. It's just . . . I don't know. One moment you're all for telephoning the police, the next you're asking me to sit down and eat with the corpse of the man I've just shot lying in the next room. It seems a little sudden, that's all.'

Gemma smiled at him over a forkful of marinated anchovies.

'It was something you said.'

'What?'

'You said, "It's something I'll be living with for the rest of my life. You too, if we're still together."'

Zen looked at her indignantly, as though she'd faulted his logic.

'Well, you will!' he said.

Gemma laughed.

'That isn't the point, silly.'

'Then what is?'

'Never mind. Shame about the mullet. It was gorgeous. Fresh off the boat.'

'We could still cook it.'

'It won't be the same when we get back.'

'Get back from what?'

'Disposing of the body, of course. We'll have to get out into deep water. That'll take hours. We couldn't be back here until tomorrow afternoon at the earliest.'

'Back from where?'

A sudden hissing behind them announced that the pasta water had boiled over. Gemma got up and busied herself with the stove. The odours of garlic and oil filled the air.

'Portunciulla. That's where Tommaso keeps his boat. Our boat. It's near La Spezia. About an hour on the autostrada, depending on traffic.'

'But how are we going to get there?'

'My car has a back seat that folds down to make luggage space. He'll fit in there.'

Zen sat there, nibbling squid, sipping wine and thinking all this over with a clarity he found alarming.

'Can you operate the boat?' he asked.

Gemma waved impatiently.

'No, but you must be able to. You're Venetian, you told me.'

'Of course I can!' Zen retorted proudly. 'What sort is it?'

'A motor cruiser. The latest model, all the latest gadgets. Even I could probably drive it if I had to. A child could.'

Zen considered some more.

'We'll need to wrap the body. Do you have any spare sheets or anything like that?'

'Tons.'

Gemma did more things near the cooker and the sink, then returned with a broad dish which she set down on the table with the air of someone who is quietly satisfied with her work. Just like I did after killing Lessi, thought Zen. The dish contained a heap of *penne rigate* dressed with chopped aubergines, green olives, basil, capers and anchovies in a light tomato sauce tangy with garlic and chilli. Zen suddenly realized that he was famished.

'So how much did he tell you?' he asked as Gemma served the pasta.

'Pretty much everything, I think. He seemed to want to tell someone, to show off how brave and clever he'd been.'

'But that was all?'

'All?'

'I mean, he just tied you up. He didn't . . .'

Gemma laughed.

'No, no. Nothing like that. I don't think he was interested in women, to tell you the truth. You can usually tell, even if you're dealing with a maniac. No, the one he wanted was you. Apparently he'd tried five times, but you hadn't come across. So he was getting pretty frustrated and desperate.'

'Well, he made his move, and it still didn't take.'

'Thanks to me.'

'Yes, you were pretty good in there. So what did he tell you?'

'Well, there was the bomb in Sicily, obviously. Are you really a detective? You don't seem the type.'

'That's the key to my success, such as it is. What about the others, the people he mistook for me?'

'Apparently he got chatting with one of those African traders who work the beach, and offered him a small fortune in exchange for borrowing his robes and stock of trinkets for the day. The man jumped at the chance, of course, and as an illegal immigrant he would never dream of going to the police after he learned what had happened. Then our friend blacked up with boot polish and hit the beach. The make-up wasn't that convincing, he said, but then "no one looks at those *vucumprà* anyway". When he got to Franco's, there was a man lying face down asleep in the place you always used. He'd been watching you for days, apparently. So he walked over, as though trying to interest the man in a sale, shot him once through the heart with that silenced gun, and then tossed the man's towel over his back to cover up the wound and shuffled away. No one took the slightest notice, he said.'

She pushed her plate back.

'I'll tell you the rest later. We'd better get moving. I'm nervous suddenly, thinking of him lying in there.'

Zen ate a final forkful of the pasta, then glanced at his watch.

'What time does it get light now?' he asked.

Gemma shrugged.

'About five? Five-thirty, maybe.'

'Then we have plenty of time. Let's aim to get to the boat around four. But if you're feeling anxious, we could do some of the preliminary work. If you're still sure you want to do this, that is.'

He paused significantly. Gemma nodded. Zen made a little conciliatory gesture, as though the whole thing had been her idea in the first place.

'Fine. Let me have a cigarette, then we'll make a start.'

He smiled at her.

'Thank you for the meal. It was delicious.'

'It would have been even better with the mullet.'

'Don't worry about that. Like they say, there are plenty of good fish in the sea.'

Gemma stood up and started to clear the dishes.

'Not at our age,' she said.

It was dark outside when they started. Zen closed the shutters on the dining-room windows, then bent over Lessi's corpse and started removing the man's clothes while Gemma fetched the sheets. In the event of the body itself being discovered, Zen wanted no identifying material of any kind to be turned up at the scene. He searched the garments, but found nothing except some money which he pocketed. Then he turned to the body.

Lessi's nine-millimetre pistol must have been loaded with the same fragmenting shells that he'd used to kill Massimo Rutelli, for there were no exit wounds in the skull. The only sign of injury, apart from the superficial wounds to Lessi's scalp, was a trickle of blood from the mouth and the deep scratches inflicted by the rose thorns. It was seeing his victim naked that disturbed Zen most. He was normally un-squeamish about the dead, but Lessi's nudity he found prob-lematic. It somehow entitled him to the status of a helpless and vulnerable baby. He felt instinctively protective towards the man he had just killed, and wanted to get him covered up as soon as possible.

Gemma returned with the sheets, and then gathered up the scattered roses to clear the floor.

'I've been wanting to get rid of these for years,' she said, spreading out the two layers of pale green cotton. 'A wedding gift from one of Tommaso's aunts.'

She took Lessi's ankles, Zen his shoulders, and together they shifted the body on to the sheeting. They then folded the flap at each end up over the feet and head, and rolled the corpse to one side to make a neat bundle which Zen secured with the lengths of rope that Gemma had been tied up with. She meanwhile fetched some plastic garbage bags into which they stuffed Lessi's shoes, clothing, the wig and false moustache, along with the roses. The pistol and the Ministe-rial communication device Zen put in his pockets.

'Will there be anyone at the marina at this hour?'

'There's always someone there, to guard the property and the boats.'

'Call and tell them . . .'

He broke off.

'What if your husband is using the boat?'

'He won't be. He hardly ever uses it, and then only for trips around the bay to show off to his business friends. He gets sea-sick if there's the slightest movement.'

'All right. Call the marina and tell them that you'll be arriv-ing with a friend to take the boat out in the early hours of the morning. Say we're off to Corsica and want to make an early start. Oh, and ask them to top up the fuel and water.'

Gemma was heading into the living room when he had another thought.

'Is there an anchor on the boat?'

'Of course. Two, in fact.'

He waved her away and paced the room, thinking over his provisional plan and failing to find any obvious flaw in it. But they would get only one chance.

'That's done,' Gemma said, coming back. 'Now what?'

'Now we wait a while, until everyone around here is sound asleep. When will that be?'

'Most of them probably are already. Lucca is not really a nightlife town, apart from the kids who hang around Piazza Napoleone. This neighbourhood is very quiet.'

'Where's your car parked?'

'Just down the street.'

'Can you back it up to the door?'

'Of course.'

Zen emitted a long sigh.

'Good. We'll wait a while to make sure that everyone is settled down. The really tricky bit is going to be getting the body and the other stuff into the car. Once we're under way, barring unforeseen circumstances, it should be fairly straightforward. But if someone sees us humping an oddly shaped bundle out of here in the middle of the night, they'll remember it. And if a police patrol car happens to pass by, they're going to check.'

Back in the kitchen, Gemma poured herself some more wine and lit a cigarette.

'If anyone does notice, we're loading up a very valuable rug that I'm giving my sister for her birthday,' she said.

'At this hour?'

'Yes. She lives in Milan and we want to be back by evening.'

Zen nodded sceptically.

'It might work.'

'Of course it will.'

'Unless I'm wrong, and Lessi did have a back-up plan.'

'How do you mean?'

'Those "friends in the business" he claimed to have. He

might just have told one of them to send someone to this address if he hadn't called a certain number by a certain time. Something like that. But there's nothing we can do about that.'

'He had friends all right,' Gemma said. 'That's how he found out that you were going to America.'

Zen gazed at her.

'He did?'

She nodded.

'He also had some equipment, or code words, or access to some computers. I didn't understand all the details, but his friends told him that you were going to the States, and also the number and date of the flight you were booked on. Apparently he told them that he just wanted to confront you and "gain closure". In reality, he reckoned that was his last chance of getting even with you for what you'd done to his partner or whatever he was. Once you'd landed in America, you'd be whisked off into some secure accommodation pending the trial, and his contacts would be no use to him there. So everything depended on getting to you before that.'

'And he booked himself on the same flight and attacked me in that street in Reykjavík. But supposing the plane hadn't been diverted? What was he going to do then?'

Gemma shook her head.

'No, you don't understand. He didn't buy a ticket on the plane. He travelled as one of the cabin attendants.'

Zen laughed.

'That's impossible!'

She looked at him gravely.

'No, it wasn't. And that's what scares me most about this insane affair I suddenly find myself caught up in. It wasn't impossible at all. For people like that, and he isn't the only one by any means, nothing is impossible.'

'But how could he get through security? They must know who's going to be on any given flight. You can't just show up and be allowed on.'

'With the computer codes he had, he accessed the Alitalia database and got the details of the designated crew for the flight you were going to be on. Then he looked up the personal details, addresses and telephone numbers of male cabin attendants on the roster, discovered one who lived in Rome, and called him saying that a mutual friend had said they ought to get together. They went out to some gay club in the suburbs, then back home to the man's apartment. He didn't say what happened after that, except that he took the man's uniform and ID and changed the photo to one of him. That got him through security at Malpensa.'

'But surely the other members of the crew would have recognized that he wasn't . . . whatever his name was.'

'Enrico, I think. Yes, but once he was past security he didn't pretend to be Enrico any more. He was now someone else, who stepped in at the last moment because Enrico was ill. He'd got the story about the job out of Enrico at the club the night before. Everyone likes talking about their work. He wasn't assigned to the cabin you were in, but once the lights had been dimmed for the movie he made his way there and placed a glass of water on the tray table of the seat number you had been assigned. Everyone always drinks any water available on an aeroplane, he said.'

'Except it wasn't me, and it wasn't water.'

'Exactly. You'd switched seats, so the person who'd taken yours drank the water, which contained some high-tech poison they supplied to that undercover unit he was in. Apparently it simulates the effects of a heart attack. But he didn't want to end up in the US, where he'd done some work assignments in the past and might be recognized by the agents who were expecting you, so he sabotaged half the toilets on the plane by bunging the pillows and blankets they hand out at night down them, and then drew the senior steward's attention to the problem. That forced a diversion. He'd got this idea from some story Enrico told him, he said.'

'Enrico sounds to have been good value for a couple of drinks and a blow job.'

Gemma grimaced.

'I think the experience cost him rather more than that. Lessi was obviously a psychotic. Human life meant nothing whatever to him. Anyway, when the plane landed in Iceland, he changed into the civilian clothes he had brought with him and slipped through immigration using a false passport he had "lost" before leaving the police.'

'So it was he who attacked me in the street that night.'

'Yes. He claimed it was a total coincidence. The earlier flights back to Europe were all fully booked, so he had to wait for a late-night one. He went into town and was wandering around when he happened to catch sight of you. He said that you were drunk.'

'Iceland has that effect on you.'

'Of making you drunk?'

'Of making you need to get drunk.'

'I see. Anyway, that didn't work either, so he flew back here, assuming that you were safely out of his reach in America. Then one of his contacts got in touch and told him that your trip had been cancelled and that you were coming back to Italy. He knew your address in Rome, of course, and went to visit you there.'

She walked over and closed the window.

'Right, now I think it's time that you told me all about yourself, Dottor Zen.'

'All?'

'Everything. I think I deserve that, don't you? Under the circumstances.'

'Yes, of course. I'm just not sure where to begin.'

'How about the beginning? What's your first name, for a start?'

'Aurelio.'

She turned and beamed at him.

'What a lovely name! Go on.'

'Ah. Right. Well . . .'

This was by far the hardest thing that Zen had had to do so far that evening. He hated talking about himself. At first, he planned to give Gemma a heavily edited version of the truth, but much to his amazement he found himself telling her everything, precisely as she had asked.

She didn't even have to ask follow-up questions in the end, although she prodded him fairly hard in the initial stages. But a point came when she got up and made a large pot of coffee, turning her back on him and generating the usual amount of noise, and he just went on talking anyway. He couldn't stop!

But finally he did.

'Now it's your turn,' he told Gemma, who was sipping a mug of strong espresso opposite him at the table.

'No, no. You'll have to find out bit by bit.'

'But I told *you* everything!' he protested.

'You had to.'

'I didn't.'

'Yes, you did. Otherwise I'd have called the police and told *them* everything.'

He laughed.

'It's a bit late for that.'

'No it isn't. Even tomorrow wouldn't be too late. Or the day after that. You have Lessi's gun. You murdered him and then threatened me with the same if I didn't agree to help you dispose of his body. I think they'd believe that. Particularly if some of Lessi's friends are as vindictive as you suggest.'

Zen felt dazed, shocked, stunned by the wine and jolted by the coffee.

'You're going to tell them that?' he asked.

Gemma laughed.

'Of course not, silly. I'm just explaining the balance of power around here. You have to do what I say, but I don't have to do what you say.'

Zen thought about this for a moment, then smiled at her.

'I'll be delighted to do whatever you say.'

Gemma stood up, came round the table and kissed him lightly on the forehead.

'Good. Then let's get going.'

While Gemma went to fetch the car, taking the two rubbish bags and a couple of old coats with her, Zen dragged the bundled body of Roberto Lessi across the dining room and through to the hallway. He opened the front door to the apartment and peered out. The light had automatically extinguished itself and the entire building was silent. Then he heard a clicking sound on the steps and Gemma reappeared.

'All set,' she said.

They lifted the bundle and carried it out on to the landing, leaving the door open to provide background lighting, then down the stairs. The car was parked right in front of the main door, the hatchback open. They heaved the body inside, next to the garbage bags, and spread the coats out over it. Then Gemma ran back upstairs and locked up, while Zen climbed into the passenger seat.

A circuit of the back streets of Lucca, deserted at this time of night, brought them to one of the gates through the enormous walls, and out on to the broad avenue that circumvented the city. Five minutes after that, they had left Italy and were on the motorway.

Years before, when he had finally accepted that his daddy would never come home again, Zen had used to calm himself to sleep by imagining that his bed was in a cabin of one of those international sleeping cars which his father had once showed him in the shunting yards near Santa Lucia station, all dark wood and velvet curtains and brass-shaded lamps and a bell to ring if you needed anything. The train was making its way through a landscape filled with dangers of every kind – battles and floods and towns ablaze – but inside everything was calm. The hideous scenes visible through the window, if you were bold enough to raise the blind a crack, merely emphasized your own seclusion and safety. Meanwhile, the wheels kept ticking along over the rail joints, clickety clack, clickety clack . . .

Although Zen rarely drove if he could possibly help it, the neutral, extraterritorial domain of the *rete autostradale* never failed to have a similar calming effect on him. For the modest price of the toll, you were admitted to a private club that stretched the length and breadth of the country, a club that displayed an aristocratic disdain for regional traditions or quirks of topography, and was just about the only institution in the country guaranteed to be open twenty-four hours a day, every day of the year. Whether you were just outside Turin or two thousand metres up in the Abruzzi mountains, the same rules applied and the same facilities were available. The real world stopped at the toll gates, its limits clearly marked by the chain-link fencing. Viewed from within that boundary, the scene was at best picturesque and at worst uninspiring. In that farmhouse over there, its one wan light just showing through the storm-whipped windbreak, the father might be beating his wife and screwing his daughters, with two bodies buried in the cellar and a crazed aunt chained up in the attic. It didn't matter, that was another world. Pretty soon there would be another all-night service station where you could get a hot snack and a cold drink, buy a newspaper or a cassette tape, make a phone call and catch up on the TV news.

Gemma drove prudently, keeping well within the speed limit as they passed through the tunnels and across the long viaducts of the A11 through the southern foothills of the Apuan Alps, and then cruised down the long curved section reaching down to the coastal plain to join the main north–south motorway at Viareggio. Traffic was heavier here, mostly foreign truckers getting a head start on their long itinerary before the tourists started clogging the road later in the morning. They glided effortlessly past the big rigs, the green kilometre signs ticking off their progress. A pert crescent moon peeked archly out over the mountain chain to the east.

'Someone knew,' said Zen at last, breaking their long silence.

'Knew what?'

'Or at least suspected,' Zen continued, working out the thought which had suddenly come to him. 'And not Brugnoli. He thinks he's a player, but he's not. On the contrary, they're using him.'

Gemma took her eyes off the road for an instant to glance at him.

'When you've got a moment, would you mind telling me what on earth you're talking about?'

Zen remained silent for another minute or so, then shifted in his seat to reach his cigarettes.

'My new job,' he said, lighting up and opening the window slightly.

'What about it?'

'I couldn't understand why they had bothered to go to all that trouble, supposedly setting up this new division and making me the "founder member". They could easily have pressured me into early retirement if they'd wanted to, even produced a fake report from some doctor which diagnosed me as unfit for active service. But that didn't suit them, because someone suspected, just as Lessi did, that I knew more than I was letting on. And once I left the service, they would have no further hold over me. I could sell my story to the newspapers, even write a book about it.'

He laughed.

'As it is, they'll never let me retire! At least not until the whole cast has changed and no one cares any more.'

'Cares about what?'

Zen finished his cigarette and let the butt slide into the slipstream, then closed the window.

'That bomb attack in Sicily, the one which almost killed me? Until this evening, I thought the Mafia were responsible. I honestly did. I couldn't remember anything much about the events leading up to it. One of the doctors told me that memory loss about events preceding an incident like that is quite normal. Apparently survivors of severe car crashes usually have no idea how they happened. Mind that truck.'

'Leave the driving to me, please.'

'Sorry. Anyway, I accepted the official line about the bomb. And so did everyone else, as far as I knew. But we now know that there was at least one exception.'

'Our friend in the back.'

Zen nodded.

'But someone else must have known, too. Someone higher up the hierarchy, with enough clout to have me moved to a position where I would be safely out of the way, but still under control.'

They drove on in silence for a while.

'In which case, this person might also know that Lessi was planning to kill you.'

Zen shook his head decisively.

'No, no. The person I mean operates at a different level. He's probably someone quite high up in the *carabinieri* or the Defence Ministry. His only thought was to protect the reputation of his force. They dumped Lessi, knowing he wouldn't talk, but they weren't so sure about me.'

'So won't they get curious when Lessi mysteriously vanishes?'

'I think it'll be a relief, quite frankly. Anyway, Lessi's murderous little plot was quite clearly a personal matter. He wanted to get even, both for what had happened to his career and also for what happened to Alfredo Ferraro, who may have been his partner in more than just a professional sense. No, he'll have kept his private vendetta to himself, I'm sure of that.'

In reality, he was a lot less sure than he sounded.

At Magra, just before the turn-off for La Spezia, they stopped for a coffee. While Gemma bought some salami, cheese and rolls to see them through the rest of the morning, Zen lifted the garbage bags containing Lessi's personal effects out of the car and carried them round to the rear of the service station. He opened one of the big dumpsters and tossed the bags inside. A broken pallet was leaning against the wall. He pulled off one of the lateral slats and used it to push the bags down, then to collapse a mound of stinking rubbish over the top of them.

Gemma returned to the car with the plastic bag of provisions. She looked flustered.

'You're never going to believe this, but I just ran into someone I used to know!' she blurted out, spinning the car round in reverse and heading off to rejoin the main highway.

'Who?'

'Oh, an old boyfriend. He came up while I was waiting at the cash register. Wanted to chat.'

'What did you say?'

'I gave him the story we agreed earlier, about going to see my sister. I couldn't think of anything else on the spur of the moment.'

To his surprise, Zen found himself more jealous than worried.

'How old?'

'What?'

'The boyfriend.'

Gemma laughed harshly as the headlights devoured the darkness before them.

'Oh for God's sake! But he knows.'

'Knows what?'

'That I was here, in the middle of the night.'

'Going to see your sister.'

'But I'm not.'

Zen patted her knee in a reassuring rather than erotic way.

'Don't worry. It doesn't matter. Your ex-boyfriend doesn't matter. Neither does your husband, who'll find out sooner or later that we used his boat. None of them matters as long as we keep our wits about us and our mouths shut. The only people who can betray us are us. The rest is just hearsay.'

They ran into the roadblock the other side of La Spezia, rounding a sharp bend on a minor *strada statale* high above the glimmering sea to their left. A blue *carabinieri* jeep was parked beside the road and a uniformed officer stood on the median line waving a wand with a reflective red circular tip.

Zen swore loudly. Gemma braked to a halt. The officer approached the driver's window while his colleague watched from the car, speaking rapidly on the radio.

'Your documents, please.'

Zen handed over his personal identity card, Gemma her driving licence. The officer stepped back and scanned them by the light of his torch.

'Where are you going?' he demanded.

'To Portunciulla,' Gemma replied.

'Why so late?'

'We have a boat at the marina there. We're off to Corsica for a few days and we want to make an early start.'

The officer shone his torch into the interior of the car.

'What's that in the back?'

'Just stuff we need for our cruise,' said Gemma.

'Open it up.'

Gemma gave Zen a panicked look as she pulled a latch under the dashboard. Zen got out and walked back on the opposite side of the car from the *carabiniere*, who opened the hatchback and shone his torch inside. He swept aside the coats covering the bundled form of Roberto Lessi's corpse.

'What's that?' he demanded.

'Spars,' Zen replied. 'And a new mizzen sail. What's all this about, if you don't mind my asking?'

The officer stared suspiciously at Zen's linen suit, then slammed the hatchback shut again.

'Bank robbery in La Spezia. We're checking all the roads out of town. What's a mizzen sail?'

Zen smiled the smile of a man who is glad to have been asked that.

'It's the small triangular sail set aft on a ketch. Very much like a jib, only mounted on a boom. Its main function is to increase stability when sailing close to the wind, particularly when . . .'

The officer handed him back their documents.

'All right, all right,' he said wearily. 'You can go.'

As if by mutual agreement, they drove off in total silence until they had rounded the next hairpin bend. Then Gemma let out a long, almost silent scream.

'I don't know how much more of this I can take.'

'Plenty. You're as tough as an ox. Besides, there was no real danger. Those lads were just bored. We were probably the first vehicle to come along for an hour. I've done roadblocks myself, many years ago. It's a hell of a job. Either the car you stop is not the one you're looking for, in which case the whole thing is a waste of time, or it is, in which case you stand a good chance of getting run over or shot.'

'How do you know all those nautical words you dazzled him with?'

'I told you, I'm from Venice. It's in our blood. We drink it in with our mother's milk.'

Twenty minutes later, they reached the village of Portunci-ulla. Judging by what Zen could make out from the car, it had once been a small fishing port, but had now been taken over by holiday lets, second homes and the pleasure-boat business. The marina was situated on the northern side of the original harbour, a series of floating docks lit by overhead floodlights and protected by an artificial breakwater. Gemma stopped at the gate and identified herself to a scruffy youth with a gormless expression. He nodded slowly and vaguely, as though remembering some incident from a previous life. Then he went inside the concrete hut he had emerged from and returned with a set of keys.

'You'll be needing a hand with your stuff,' he said, pointing to the rear of the car.

'No thanks, we can manage,' Gemma replied crisply, slipping him a ten-thousand-lire note. 'Did you refuel the boat?'

'All taken care of,' the youth replied listlessly.

Gemma drove through the car park to the landward end of one of the docks, then turned and parked so that the car was in shadow. They both got out. The youth was standing at the door of his hut, watching them.

'You stay here and mind the luggage,' Gemma told Zen. 'I'll take the groceries and open up the boat, then come back with a cart for our friend in the back.'

She turned away into the shadows leading down to the dock. Zen lit a cigarette and watched her walk along the pier and board one of the motor cruisers moored there. What a piece of luck, he thought. What an incredible piece of luck! Whoever would have thought it?

'Look at the moon!' said a voice behind him. *'Quant'è bella!'*

He turned to find the scruffy youth gazing at him with an ecstatic expression. Zen did not reply.

'It's always beautiful,' the youth went on earnestly, 'but we can't always see it.'

'No.'

'And even when we can, half the time we don't.'

'How very true.'

The youth strode up to him and grasped his right arm tightly.

'Just imagine if the moon only came out every fifty years, like an eclipse of the sun. People all over the world would stay up all night to look at it, dancing and singing and weeping for joy!'

'Quite possibly.'

The rapt expression vanished from the youth's face like a patch of condensation off glass.

'But it's there all the time,' he continued in a voice drained of all emotion. 'It's staring us in the face, so we take it for granted.'

Zen threw away his spent cigarette.

'An interesting thought,' he said.

The youth was now gazing in through the rear window of the car. The shrouded body seemed to glow in the moonlight.

'It's right there in front of us, so we don't even see it,' he murmured in the same affectless tone.

'Mmm.'

He turned to Zen with a piercingly intense stare.

'Maybe that's why we don't see God either.'

Zen heard a rumbling sound. Gemma was wheeling a small handcart along the dock. He peeled off some money and handed it to the youth.

'Listen, I've just realized that we forgot to bring any matches with us. Stupid mistake, but it's the kind of little thing that can ruin your holiday. Do you think you could find us some? Or a lighter. Keep the change.'

The youth nodded dolefully and headed back to his hut as Gemma emerged from the shadows.

'I forgot to tell you about Piero,' she said. 'He's a bit odd.'

'He's a lunatic, in the literal sense of the word, and he'll be back any moment. Let's get the stiff on the cart, then I'll take it down while you deal with him. Tell him you're Astarte. He'll obey your every command.'

He opened the hatchback and hauled Lessi's body half out of the car, then lifted it on to the trolley. Piero was already on his way back. Zen grabbed the handles and started to make his way down the path to the dock. Unfortunately the baggage cart, although built to carry heavy loads, was not designed to accommodate anything long and unstable. Halfway down the slope, one of the wheels hit a rock, the body slewed to one side and the whole thing overturned.

Before Zen could react, the youth had bounded up and started to lift Lessi's feet.

'Turn the cart over,' he said. 'I'll help you load it back on.'

'That's all right, we can manage.'

'No, no! It's nothing.'

Zen set the cart back on its wheels, then lifted Lessi's head. Together they set the bundle back in place.

'Whew, that's heavy,' said Piero.

Zen nodded distractedly.

'What's inside?' the youth enquired.

'A human corpse. My late brother-in-law. We're going to take him out to sea and throw him overboard. Saves a fortune on the funeral expenses.'

Piero gazed at Zen with a look of growing anger.

'You think I'm crazy, don't you?'

'No, I think you're brilliantly sane, but who cares what I think?'

Gemma materialized between them and turned the youth away, her arm around his shoulders.

'I'm sorry, Piero,' Zen heard her say. 'We've both had a long hard day planning this trip and we haven't slept. It was very kind of you to prepare the boat and give us the keys, and I'll tell the management what a good job you did when I . . .'

As she led Piero back towards his hut, Zen hefted the handles of the cart and continued down the path and on to the dock, where Gemma rejoined him.

'Are you out of your mind?' she hissed in a hoarse whisper.

'Probably we both are. It's just that you're handling it better.'

'If he tells anyone what you said, we're each facing a life sentence.'

'I'm sorry, I just snapped. But don't worry, no one's going to pay any attention to what Piero tells them.'

'They'd better not.'

'Of course they won't.'

Once again, he was a lot less sure than he sounded.

Gemma didn't reply, and for a while Zen thought that she was furious with him, or understandably scared at the magnitude of what she had got herself into. But when she did speak, it was in a mild, relaxed tone.

'This one,' she said, nodding towards a huge teak motor cruiser bristling with chrome and brass fittings. Zen pushed the cart along the dock, stopping beside a short set of metal steps leading up to the afterdeck.

'Ready?' he said.

Gemma nodded. Together they lugged the increasingly stiff body of Roberto Lessi off the cart and up to the steps. Gemma went aboard while Zen lifted the cadaver so that it was vertical, then hoisted it up by the feet while Gemma hauled it over the side. They had just succeeded in getting the centre of gravity inboard when the sound of splashing water drew their attention to the yacht in the next berth, where a man dressed only in a nautical cap, a blue blazer with brass buttons, and the lower half of a woman's bikini was urinating off the stern.

'What you got there?' he asked in a slurred voice.

'Freshly killed meat,' Zen replied.

He heard Gemma's intake of breath, and glanced quickly up at her as he raised himself up on the first of the steps and heaved the bundle over the side. He turned back to their neighbour with a broad smile.

'A whole *porchetta*. Some friends of ours are having a party at their villa up the coast and this is our contribution. Slaughtered a couple of days ago and then slow-roasted over a wood fire by a real artisan up in the mountains.'

The man adjusted the bikini bottom and sniffed loudly.

'Mmm! I can smell the stuffing from here. Wish I had friends like that. All mine have passed out, one of them on the lavatory. Hence the public display. Care for a drink?'

'No thanks, Arnaldo,' Gemma replied. 'We want to make an early start.'

'Suit yourselves.'

He pointed an admonitory finger at Zen.

'She tends to slew to one side a bit when the revs are low. Can make getting in and out tricky. Get all lined up and then give her all you've got. A word to the wise. *Buon viaggio.*'

He staggered down the companionway and disappeared.

Zen climbed aboard and looked at Lessi's body lying collapsed on the deck.

'Let's get this stowed inside,' he said.

Gemma opened the doors to the main saloon. They carried the body through and laid it out on a row of bench seating. Zen placed Lessi's pistol in a knife drawer in the galley, and they returned to the afterdeck.

'All right,' said Zen. 'Time to go. Tell me when to cast off.'

Gemma regarded him with a puzzled expression.

'Me? I told you I don't know how to drive this thing. Tommaso always did that, when he did it at all. He would never let me near any of the little knobs and levers.'

Zen gave a world-weary smile.

'Wonderful,' he said.

Gemma leant over and kissed him on the cheek.

'Never mind! You'll do just fine. You're from Venice, remember? It's in your blood. You drank it in with your mother's milk.'

Zen glared at her.

'Give me the keys and let go the mooring ropes.'

In the end, handling the boat turned out to be quite simple. All the controls in the cockpit mounted above the aft deck were marked with large metal plates clearly designed with the sort of people who bought these floating mobile homes in mind. Zen turned on the navigation lights and then the engine, which started immediately and settled into a low, reassuring growl. Gemma threw the lines on board and then scampered up the ladder, hauling it up after her. Once they were clear of the dock, Zen applied just enough reverse thrust and port wheel to bring the bow round, then engaged forward gear and minimal throttle while they glided slowly down the twin lines of moored boats. Once they were in the channel beyond, he brought the vessel round and revved up slightly. He didn't notice any tendency to slew to either side. Or had Arnaldo been referring to something else?

He steered past the end of the breakwater and out into the open sea beyond. The darkness was suddenly immense.

'Where are we going?' asked Gemma, appearing in the cockpit beside him and lighting a cigarette.

'Somewhere the water's deep. I don't suppose there's such a thing as a chart aboard.'

Gemma clicked her fingers decisively.

'Ah! Now that I do know about. Tommaso got it a few months before we split up. In fact I think it may well have been one of the reasons why. You know, those little niggly details that suddenly make you realize what you've known all along, namely that you're living with a complete jerk.'

'The chart, *cara*. You can tell me about your love life later.'

Gemma pushed a button on a video screen mounted to Zen's left. It flickered and then settled into a discreet glow.

'*Il mio caro sposo* was a boy-toy fanatic. If he's talked me through this box of tricks once, he must have done it a dozen times. He just couldn't get over the fact that I couldn't get as excited about it as him.'

'I'm not interested in video games! I want a chart to the waters we're in, before we hit some reef and end up as dead as our stowaway.'

'This is a chart. I mean, all the charts are on here. There's a menu, but the default one – the one that's showing now – will be the one you want. You jiggle this button here and then click this, and lo and behold a blob appears. That shows where we are. Then you move the cursor to where you want to go, like this, and click again. The dotted line shows you the course you've chosen.'

'That one cuts across the tip of the peninsula.'

'Then choose another. After that you press here, where it says "Set Course", and then here, "Engage Automatic Pilot". After that, it's just a matter of deciding how fast you want to go and keeping an eye out for other boats. Would you like some coffee?'

'I'd love one. With a shot of grappa, if there is any.'

'Of course there is. Tommaso was a complete bastard, but he didn't cheap out. There's everything. Microwave, Jacuzzi, satellite TV, sound-surround stereo, DVD player, computers with Internet access, and of course a fully stocked bar.'

She turned to leave. Zen stopped her with one finger placed just above her left breast.

'Won't he be angry when he finds out?' he asked.

'Finds out about what?'

'That we've taken his boat without his permission.'

Gemma smiled radiantly and kissed him very briefly on the lips.

'I certainly hope so,' she said.

Zen throttled back, leaving just enough power to maintain steerage way, and studied the video screen more closely. It showed a detailed nautical chart of the Gulf of La Spezia, the white blob indicating their current position just off the coast at Portunciulla. He wiggled the button until the arrow lay over the entrance to the gulf to the south-west, then clicked the button Gemma had showed him. The dotted line reappeared. He inspected it closely. There were no marked rocks or other obstructions. He pressed the other two buttons. The dotted line became continuous, and the boat nudged round gently to starboard, then settled on the new course. 'SSW 15.8' read the display on the screen. Zen checked the compass. That was indeed the heading. He increased the engine power until the wavelets under the bow produced a healthy smacking sound, then settled back and lit a cigarette.

Gemma brought Zen his *caffè corretto* and seated herself in the other leather-clad stool in the cockpit.

'Aren't you having anything?' he asked.

She shook her head.

'Actually, I think I might take a nap, if that's all right with you. I'm pretty exhausted.'

As yet there was no sign of daybreak, but the jagged promontory to their right and the imposing mountain chain on the other side stood out velvet black in the incisive moonlight. All around, the undulating surface of the water stirred and shifted restlessly in continual permutations of some underlying pattern always alluded to but never stated. There were no other vessels in sight, and the only light was the insistent blinking of a lighthouse on the Isola del Tino at the very end of the peninsula.

'Well, I'm going to lie down,' said Gemma.

'*Sogni d'oro.*'

Zen settled back into the comfortable chair, sipping his stiffened espresso, and watched the coastline slide past. Unlike Gemma, he didn't feel tired at all, but exhilarated and about twenty years younger. They'd done it! He'd never really believed they would until now, but they had. The boat was at sea, Lessi's body safely on board, and as far as he knew no paper trail behind them. Once they got into deeper water, he would detach one of the boat's anchors, hitch it up to a spare rope, tie that around the corpse and heave the whole issue overboard. Then he'd toss the gun in after it, and they would be in the clear. No one could ever find out what had really happened.

Despite his apparent wakefulness, he must have dozed slightly, because he was summoned back to full consciousness by a beeping sound. At first he thought it was the secret communication device he had been given at the Ministry, but when he checked in his pocket the unit proved to be dormant. Then he realized that it was coming from the navigation screen on the ledge in front of him, signalling that they had arrived at the position previously entered.

By now it was almost light, one of those long, slow, summer dawns full of promise. Zen picked a point at random on the chart, far out in the Ligurian Sea, then confirmed the course and clicked the autopilot button. The boat obediently bobbed round to the west and thudded forward into the slightly steeper seas. He checked the horizon. A few sets of navigation lights were showing out in the main sea lane, but all at a considerable distance. He rubbed the slight chill of dawn off his hands and went below.

Inside the saloon, Gemma was lying quietly asleep under a blanket on the row of seating opposite Lessi's bundled body. They both looked very cosy. With the boat's computer systems apparently doing all the work, Zen was strongly tempted to join them, but resisted the impulse. Instead he found the bag of groceries and took it into the spacious galley, where he made himself a salami roll. He then removed a couple of cans of beer from the fridge and made his way back to the cockpit.

And it was just as well he did, for around the time he finished the roll and the first can of beer, the engine's reassuringly sexy murmur became raucous and intermittent, and shortly after that stopped altogether. The boat came to a halt, slurping and sloshing around at random in the shallow waves.

Zen grabbed the second can of beer and took a long pull. His knowledge of engines of any kind was strictly limited to knowing how to turn them on and off. This one had already turned itself off, though, and showed no inclination to start again no matter how many times he twisted the ignition key or pushed the starter button. He had no idea how to work the marine radio, either, still less what frequencies to use. Which left them adrift on a lee shore a couple of kilometres off the Tuscan coast, in water too shallow to risk disposing of Lessi's corpse. Sooner or later it would turn up in a fishing net or washed up by the currents on a beach, and then the investigation would begin. If that ever happened, Zen had no illusions about how it would end. His only hope – *their* only hope – was to ensure that it never started in the first place.

He tried his mobile phone, but couldn't get a signal. Using the Ministry's much-vaunted emergency device was clearly out of the question. The same applied to putting out a Mayday call on the radio, even supposing he could get it to work. The coastguards would eventually send someone out to tow them into port, but with Lessi's body still aboard. But if he didn't, they were bound to be spotted in the end by some passing boat or plane, with the same result. And if even that failed, the wind and waves would eventually carry the boat ashore.

Shallow water or not, then, the first priority was to get the murdered man overboard. He ferreted about in various drawers and cupboards until he found a heavy screwdriver that would serve as a marlinspike, then made his way out on deck. One of the vessels he had spotted earlier was a lot closer now. Not only that, but it seemed to be coming directly towards them. There wasn't a moment to lose.

The twin anchors, of the modern plough design, were stowed inboard at the bow. Both were attached to lengths of neatly coiled chain. Neither showed any sign of ever having been used. If you couldn't plug in the electrics and step ashore to restock the fridge, Tommaso wouldn't have been interested. Zen inserted the screwdriver into the shackle holding one of the anchors to its chain and heaved, without the slightest effect. He looked up. The oncoming vessel was a lot closer now. It looked very much like a coastguard cutter.

He moved over to the other anchor and twisted on the screwdriver with all his might. Finally the screw gave and reluctantly started to turn. Zen forced it round until it finally cleared the shackle, then pulled out the pin, releasing the anchor. Bending his knees, he gripped the anchor with both hands, lifted it with difficulty and began to make his way back aft. As he was negotiating the narrow passage between the saloon decking and the guard rail, a freak wave hit the port bow, causing the boat to corkscrew and sending him headlong on to the deck, falling on top of the anchor with a jolt that made him cry out.

He lay there, wondering if he had cracked his newly set ribs and then realizing that he could very easily have fallen overboard and drowned. I can't do this alone, he thought. It's all too difficult. I need help.

'Do you need help?'

The voice seemed to have come from everywhere and nowhere. Deafening, raucous and only just comprehensible, it was not a kind or a pleasant voice, but it was the voice of power. Zen raised himself up on one elbow and looked over the canvas screen at the base of the guard rail. A fishing boat of some kind was lying some ten metres off to port. A man on the bridge had a large yellow megaphone in his hand.

'Do you need help?' he repeated.

Zen got up quickly.

'No, we're fine, thanks,' he yelled back, cupping a hand to his mouth. 'Thanks all the same. Much appreciated.'

A sign from the man on the bridge indicated that he couldn't hear. A moment later, the trawler reversed engines loudly, then went ahead at a slight angle to come alongside. A man dressed in a filthy green sweatshirt and jeans leapt nimbly across to the afterdeck of the motor boat.

'What's the problem?' he asked.

Zen smiled largely.

'Oh, nothing really. Just a little trouble with the engine. Once I've sorted out the gear I'll anchor and take the appropriate action.'

The man looked at him incredulously.

'How many metres of chain have you got?'

Zen, of course, hadn't a clue.

'Well . . .' he began.

'It's over fifty metres to the bottom here. The hook would never hold. Where's the motor? Let me take a look. It might be something quite simple.'

He turned and looked around, then strode into the main saloon where Gemma and Roberto Lessi lay stretched out opposite each other.

'No, wait!' Zen said feebly.

But it was too late. The man had found a recessed metal ring in one of the floorboards, and pulled it up to open a concealed hatchway down which he disappeared.

A door at the end of the saloon was open into a cabin with a large double bed. Zen went in, took a blanket from one of the closets and draped it quickly over Lessi's corpse. A moment later the trawlerman returned.

'Blockage in the fuel line,' he said, wiping his hands on his sweatshirt. 'Often happens if the boat's not used that much. It should be all right now.'

He looked around at the gaudy, vulgar luxury of the saloon.

'Sleeping soundly, your friends.'

Zen laughed.

'Yes, they are! We had a bit of a late night. So it's all working normally?'

The man headed out on deck, then ran up the steps to the cockpit and pushed the ignition button. The engine fired immediately and settled into its previous regular throb. Zen took out his wallet.

'How much do I owe you?'

'No, no, that's all right. Law of the sea, isn't it? We all help each other out. Never know when you might need it next.'

Nevertheless, he did not leave. Then Zen had an inspiration.

'Did you have good fishing?' he asked.

'Not bad.'

'Do you have a nice red mullet you could sell me?'

The man's face creased in a broad smile.

'We got some beauties. Hold on a moment.'

They went down to the afterdeck and he shouted something to one of the men on the trawler. A moment later, the other man reappeared and a large silvery-red object came flying through the air between the boats. Zen's saviour caught it neatly and laid it out on the planking.

'Still twitching,' he remarked. 'Only been out of the water an hour or so.'

'How much?'

The man shrugged.

'Whatever you think.'

Zen handed him a hundred-thousand-lire note.

'Thanks,' he said. 'It'll make a magnificent lunch.'

'*Grazie a lei, e buon appetito*,' he called, jumping back to the fishing boat, which nudged ahead and continued on its course.

Zen put the fish away in the fridge, then returned to the cockpit, engaged forward gear and revved the engine slightly. The boat obediently swung round on to its former course. He sat back on the stool and lit a cigarette, feeling pretty smug. He'd sorted everything out. It was all going to be fine.

When he finished the cigarette, he remembered that the anchor was still lying unsecured on the foredeck and went out quickly to retrieve it. A distant drone attracted his attention. To the south, a big twin-rotor military helicopter was making its way up the coast. Zen bent down to pick up the anchor and then noticed a small rectangular black box lying just inside one of the scuppers. He recognized it immediately as the emergency communication device he had been given at the Ministry. It must have slipped out of his pocket when he fell. He bent and lifted it up, turning it to replace it. Only then did he notice that the red button on the front was glowing brightly.

It took him a moment to realize what had happened. The fall must have jarred the protective plastic cover loose, and then he had stepped on the device when he went aft to speak to the trawlerman. At which moment, at least fifteen minutes ago now, an all-points red-alert alarm call had gone out to the security services coded with the exact position of a boat carrying not just the indispensable Dottor Zen, supposedly menaced by an unknown but potentially deadly threat, but the bullet-ridden corpse of the late Roberto Lessi, late of the *carabinieri*'s elite ROS unit.

The helicopter was closer now, and heading straight towards the boat. Zen grabbed the black box and hurled it as far as he could into the sea. Please God the thing didn't work underwater. He ran back to the cockpit and gunned the motor to its maximum power. The bow leapt up and a series of increasingly rapid smashing sounds from the oncoming waves made the entire hull shake. Everything not fastened down became mobile, pens and cigarettes and Zen's coffee cup and plate spilling down off the ledge to the deck. Then the helicopter was on them, directly overhead now, the noise of its engines deafening. The boat bucked and shuddered as it slapped down the waves, turning the sea to either side into a creamy vector of foam.

'What's the hell's going on?'

The voice was Gemma's, but Zen did not turn. A moment later, she was in the cockpit with him.

'What are you doing? You're driving like a maniac!'

Zen could hear her clearly now, he realized, because the helicopter had gone, pursuing its unwavering course to the northwest. He watched it become small and insignificant, then throttled back and laughed abruptly.

'Couldn't help myself! The boy in me, you know. I just wanted to see how fast it would go.'

Gemma rolled her eyes.

'I fell off the seating and banged my head on the table leg.'

'Sorry, I wasn't thinking.'

All was quiet and calm again now.

'Apart from that, did you sleep well?'

'Like a baby. Boats always put me to sleep.'

'Always?' Zen enquired with an arch look.

'Well, almost always. How have things been here?'

'Very quiet.'

'You must be exhausted.'

'Not really. I'm enjoying myself. I'd forgotten how much fun boats are. There's always something that needs attention. Keeps you awake and alert.'

'Don't you want a rest? I'll keep lookout and call you if anything happens.'

'Not until we've disposed of our passenger.'

'And when's that going to be?'

Zen pointed to the video screen.

'When we get here. I don't know exactly how long that will be.'

Gemma pushed a button to one side of the screen and read the overlaid display.

'About forty minutes, at the present speed.'

'I can hold out till then. Particularly with another cup of coffee.'

'I'll make some.'

Forty-three minutes later the beeper on the navigational display sounded again, announcing that they had arrived at the reference point which Zen had selected. By then he had brought the anchor aft and unhitched one of the mooring lines from its cleat and rolled it up beside the anchor.

Even Tommaso's state-of-the-art echo sounder couldn't cope with the depth of water under the hull, returning only nonsensically shallow readings based on some passing shoal of fish, but according to the chart they were in a zone over three hundred metres deep. Zen cut the motor and scanned the sea around them, first with the naked eye and then the binoculars Gemma found for him. The Italian coast was a ghostly memory swathed in haze, and the only vessels in sight were two freighters and a ferry, all hull-down on the horizon.

They carried the corpse out of the saloon and laid it down on the aft decking, leaning up against the gunwale. It was stiff as a board by now, and much easier to handle. Zen climbed down the steps to the bathing deck suspended over the water aft, while Gemma levered up the other end of the body and tilted the whole thing over the edge while Zen took the weight and guided it down on to the plastic deck. He then returned for the anchor, while Gemma followed him down with the length of mooring line.

So close to the sea, the air smelt fresh and invigorating. Little wavelets splashed them from time to time as they wound the rope round and round the corpse at the neck and ankles. Zen then secured each end with a series of half-hitches and passed both through the eye of the anchor, before finishing off the job with a final set of knots and tying the two loose ends together in a reef knot. He rose, surveying his work.

'That ought to hold him.'

'Should we say something?' asked Gemma.

'Say what?'

'I don't know. Isn't there some service for a burial at sea? "We commit thy body to the waves and thy soul to Almighty God." Something like that.'

Zen grimaced.

'Let's just take care of the body part. You roll it over, I'll lift the anchor.'

They worked the bundle to the very edge of the platform, where Zen laid the anchor gently on top of it like a wreath.

'Right,' he said with a sigh of relief. 'One, two, three . . .'

The resulting splash was almost derisibly insignificant. For a few moments they were able to make out the white form spiralling down through the water, gradually shrinking and losing substance until it disappeared altogether. Gemma crossed herself.

'What about the gun?' she asked.

Zen clicked his fingers.

'Good point.'

They climbed back up the ladder to the afterdeck. Zen went into the saloon, removed Lessi's pistol from the drawer where he had stowed it, returned on deck and threw it overboard. Gemma emerged from the bathroom, where she had been washing her hands.

'What do we do now?' she asked.

Zen looked at her standing there in the sunlight with her sturdy, expectant expression. He knew exactly what he wanted to do, but it didn't seem the moment, particularly since he had not washed his hands. Then he had an idea so totally crazy that he knew at once he would have to do it.

'Let's have lunch,' he said.

Gemma wrinkled her nose.

'Motorway cheese and salami? I don't think I'm that hungry.'

'I have other plans.'

He went back up to the cockpit and consulted the chart. Yes, there it was. He clicked around, set the new course and engaged the engine. The boat nosed about towards the southeast and set about its business of showing the waves who was boss.

'Where are we going?' asked Gemma.

'I'm going to sleep. Keep an eye out for other shipping, and wake me in plenty of time if anything is getting too close.'

'All right, but where are *we* going?'

Zen smiled mysteriously.

'To prison.'

'Prison?'

He nodded.

'Like in that board game. "Go to jail. Go directly to jail."'

'What are you talking about?'

'I'll tell you later.'

Being born is confusing. Dying may well prove to be even more so. Even waking up is pretty damn confusing. Such were Aurelio Zen's initial thoughts on emerging from a seamless, dreamless sleep. Why me? Why here? Why now?

The answer to these questions, when it popped up, seemed incontrovertible. In his mindless exhaustion, he had lain down on the very spot where Roberto Lessi's body had been lying for all those hours. This surely meant bad luck. Even monks and nuns were threatening enough, their presence demanding a discreet jiggle of the testicles as an antidote against that other world of chastity. But there was no *gesto di scongiuro* effective against death, and he had been rubbing up against it for hours, and asleep, to make it worse.

But was Lessi's spirit a threat, he wondered, still lying in the shallow depression which he and his victim's corpse had made in the leather cushions. His mother had spoken to him in the apartment in Rome, but that had come as no surprise. He had always known that she had the power to get in touch with him at any time she wanted. But Lessi? 'We commit thy body to the waves and thy soul to Almighty God.' No, Lessi didn't have that kind of power, of that Zen felt certain. Maybe his friends did, though.

'They don't put the bottles in the box, they wrap the box around the bottles.' That teasing phrase was clear enough now. He had been telling himself that there was more than one solution to a problem. His mind had always worked like that, in a facetious, allusive way, but its insights usually turned out to have been correct. Too bad he hadn't understood them at the time. And what had his mother told him? 'Just don't ever turn your back on them, that's all. Don't look them in the eye and never turn your back.' She'd been right, as always. He'd got away with it this time, but as he stood up he vowed never to turn his back on anyone ever again.

It was only once he was vertical that he realized the real reason why he had woken in the first place. The boat was completely still and silent. His first thought was that the motor must have failed again, but that wouldn't explain the lack of motion. Really disturbed now, he ran out on to the afterdeck. A pile of woman's clothing lay strewn on the planking. He looked about him. The first thing he saw was land, some kind of rocky shoreline. They must have run aground, he thought guiltily. He'd fallen asleep and Gemma had somehow stranded the boat.

But where was Gemma? No sign of her in the cockpit or on deck, apart from her discarded clothing. He called her name loudly several times. No answer. God, no! Had she fallen overboard, as he himself so nearly had?

'Ciao, caro!'

The voice came from behind him, from the land. He turned and beheld through the midday heat haze the figure of Gemma waving to him from a sandy beach. Zen looked about in puzzlement. The boat appeared to be securely moored at anchor in a few metres of water in a small bay protected from such wind as there was by a low headland. The land behind the beach rose steeply in a jumble of shrubs, bushes and stunted trees. There was no sign of any paths down to the water, and no other boats in sight.

'It's lovely here,' called Gemma. 'Come on over.'

'How?'

'Swim! I did.'

'I don't have my costume.'

'Neither do I. This is underwear.'

Zen gestured vaguely. There didn't seem to be any way out. He returned to the saloon and stripped off, then ventured back out on deck. Feeling as embarrassed as a schoolboy, he climbed down the ladder to the bathing deck again, then dived in and swam ashore. The water was warm and silkily salty. He shook himself off and walked up to where Gemma was lying, then threw himself down beside her on the hot sand.

'Where on earth are we?' he demanded.

'It's called Gorgona. I noticed it coming up on the left and it just looked so gorgeous I drove over to take a closer look. Then I saw this bay, and came in and parked.'

'You should have woken me! There might have been rocks under water at the entrance. You could have wrecked the boat!'

'Well, I didn't. And isn't it wonderful? No one here, and not a single sign that anyone ever has been. It's paradise! Much nicer than wherever you were planning to take us.'

'This is where I was planning to take us.'

'But you said we were going to prison.'

'Gorgona is a prison island. That's why there's no one here.'

Gemma looked at him in alarm.

'Oh my God, I suppose they'll be round with guns any moment to arrest us for trespassing!'

'I doubt it. The prison is for inner-city juvenile riff-raff. Not the sort who have friends who might organize a getaway in a power boat. Security's pretty minimal.'

'How do you know?'

'This is where they took me after I disappeared that evening in Versilia. I thought then how wonderful it would be to come back here with you some day, but of course I never thought it would be possible.'

Gemma smiled at him.

'I didn't know you were thinking of me then.'

'Well, I was. And now I'm thinking of lunch. I bought this fish . . .'

'I found it in the fridge. How did you get it?'

'Oh, I hailed a passing fishing boat.'

She laughed.

'Like hailing a taxi?'

'Sort of. Anyway, it should be fabulous. What are we going to do with it?'

Gemma sat up and brushed the sand off her stomach. Her dark, prominent nipples showed through the wet brassiere.

'All taken care of,' she said. 'I cleaned and scaled it and set it to marinate in oil and lemon juice. It should be ready by now. Fifteen minutes or so under the grill and we can eat.'

Zen got up and walked across the beach to the bottom of the rocky slope. The soil here was blisteringly hot. He took a few painful steps, inspecting the shrubbery and rubbing the leaves occasionally, then tore off two branches and skipped back to the sand, burying his seared soles for a moment in the cooler layer beneath the surface. When he could walk normally again, he returned to Gemma and handed her the branches.

'For you,' he said with a mock bow.

She inspected the gift.

'Wild thyme and rosemary. Perfect! But it'll get ruined in the water.'

'I'll look after it. Come on, I'm starving.'

They swam back to the boat, Zen doing a back crawl with his legs alone, holding the herbs high above the water with one hand. Gemma took them from him on the bathing deck and went to shower in the impressively equipped bathroom. She reappeared wearing, judging by various subtle signs, only her outer layer of clothing.

Gemma laid a table on the afterdeck under a canvas canopy that Zen cranked down on her instructions. Then they brought out the food and some white wine which Gemma had placed in the fridge earlier. The dining space was cool, airy and delightful. They ate ravenously, mouthfuls of succulent fish and crusty bread washed down with the tart, prickly wine.

'God, this place is gorgeous!' Gemma exclaimed. 'Hard to believe that it's a prison.'

Zen nodded.

'It is, though. And we're prisoners.'

She frowned.

'You mean we can't leave? That's all right with me.'

'No, we don't have to stay here. We're prisoners on parole, free to come and go as we wish, up to a point. But prisoners just the same.'

'What are you talking about, Aurelio?'

It was the first time she had called him that. Zen laid his plate aside and lit a cigarette.

'I can't count how many cases I've dealt with that would never have been solved if one of the parties involved hadn't decided, for one reason or another, to cooperate with the police. Well, it's the same here. I've killed a man and you've helped me dispose of the body. There's a very good chance that we'll get away with it, I think, but only as long as we keep faith with one another. And I don't just mean now, in the heat of the moment, here in this paradise. I mean back there in the real world, and for ever. That's what I meant when I said that we're prisoners. Not of the state, but of each other.'

Gemma smiled mysteriously. She seemed to be considering various possible answers.

'Well, you'll just have to make sure always to be very nice to me,' she said at length.

'And vice versa.'

'But you've got more to lose. You actually shot him after all. I was tied up at the time, remember? A helpless female in peril. Anyway, the key thing is that we'll obviously have to stay closely in touch, so that we can keep an eye on each other and check that the other person isn't getting any dangerous ideas. In fact it would probably be best if you were to move in with me, for the time being at least. Otherwise I might lie awake worrying about what you were up to. I hate sleepless nights. Unless there's something better to do, of course.'

They looked at each other for a very long time. Then Gemma yawned loudly and stood up.

'All that food and wine's made me sleepy. I'm going to lie down for a bit. Come and join me, if you want.'

She went into the saloon and through into the forward

cabin, where she removed her clothes and lay down on the bed. Zen remained where he was for a moment, staring up at the sky. A skein of high cloud was drifting in from the west. The weather was changing, and not for the better. They'd need to leave soon. He tossed his cigarette into the clear blue water and followed Gemma inside.

About the Author

Michael Dibdin is the author of fourteen previous novels, including *Dead Lagoon*, *Così Fan Tutti*, *A Long Finish*, and *Blood Rain*. A native of England, he now lives in Seattle, Washington.